Wozzeck

Izdryk

Wozzeck

translated and with an introduction
by Marko Pavlyshyn

КІУС
CIUS

Canadian Institute of Ukrainian Studies Press

Edmonton 2006 Toronto

Canadian Institute of Ukrainian Studies Press

University of Alberta
Edmonton, Alberta
Canada T6G 2E8

University of Toronto
Toronto, Ontario
Canada M5T 1N7

ISBN 1–894865–06–5 (bound); ISBN 1–894865–07–3 (pbk.)

Library and Archives Canada Cataloguing in Publication

Izdryk
Wozzeck / Izdryk ; translated and with an introduction by Marko Pavlyshyn.

Translation into English of the Ukrainian work of the same title .
ISBN 1–894865–06–5 (bound).—ISBN 1–894865–07–3 (pbk.)

I. Pavlyshyn, Marko II. Title.

PG3949.19.Z37W6913 2006 891.7'934 C2006-903742-6

Publication of this volume is made possible in part by grants from the Danylo Husar Struk Memorial Fund at the Canadian Foundation for Ukrainian Studies and the Cosbild Club Endowment Fund at the Canadian Institute of Ukrainian Studies.

Printed in Canada

CONTENTS

Even in his most implausible speculations it never occurred to him that all of his experience hitherto had no weight, comprised no metaphysical capital, and was altogether unworthy of attention.
(Izdryk, *Double Leon*)[1]

INTRODUCTION

Wozzeck IV

Like most dimensions of political, social and cultural life in every part of what so suddenly ceased to be the Soviet Union, during the 1990s literature in Ukraine experienced a profound and, in part, traumatic transformation. Destabilized well before the collapse of the USSR in 1991, the ideological and aesthetic framework of socialist realism disintegrated, bringing down with it the view, traditional in East European cultures, of the arts as privileged commentators upon, and legislators for, society. Familiar cultural institutions like the Writers' Union, created half a century earlier to regulate creative activity in accordance with the propaganda requirements of the Communist Party, sought feverishly to adjust themselves to what they imagined would be the nation-building priorities of the newly independent Ukrainian state, little realizing that the emergence of market relations signaled the end of the comfortable alliance between the state and the "cultural worker." The old mechanism for the publication and distribution of books ceased to function, and in the context of economic crisis many established writers faced impoverishment. In the newly fluid—chaotic, as many believed—cultural environment, established figures found their authority set at nought, their reputations challenged, while a generation of alternative writers who had come to the fore in the late 1980s were seen by many of their older colleagues as little more than self-indulgent and irresponsible mockers of received cultural values.[2]

At the turn of the new millennium, as the dust settled on the controversies between the traditionalists and the iconoclasts, it became possible to discern the features of the new literary landscape that had emerged. The fundamental divide was, as it had been during the debate on modernism a hundred years earlier,[3] between a literature programmatically focused on Ukrainian literary traditions and the realities of contemporary Ukrainian life, on the one hand, and a literature striving for participation in a broader context, often labeled "European," on the other.[4] The divide did not overlap with a watershed between traditionalism and aesthetic innovation.[5] In each camp there were notable writers whose contributions to literature are difficult to discuss without observing their "neomodern" or "postmodern" qualities.[6] Among the cultural essentialists were, above all, the doyen of Ukrainian letters, Valerii Shevchuk (b. 1939), such prose writers as Yevhen Pashkovsky (b. 1962), Viacheslav Medvid (b. 1951), Oles Ulianenko (b. 1962) and, from a younger generation, Serhii Zhadan (b. 1974)—critical neorealists whose stylistic idiom was, however, recognizably modernist.[7] Those whose literary identity was shaped by a vision of westward cultural integration were, in the main, participants in the Ukrainian strand of a global postmodernism. This phenomenon was stimulated, in part, by transnational cultural fashion and, in part, by the appropriateness of the relativist, self-ironic and combinatorial qualities of the postmodern consciousness to the post-Soviet condition, characterized as it was by competing values and world views, newly unstable life experiences and expectations, and the ambivalent attitudes of many to the less-than-complete demise of Soviet cultural colonialism.[8]

Ukrainian postmodernism developed with a distinctly regional flavor. Several of its representatives emphatically identified themselves and their movement with western Ukraine, claiming a cultural affinity with Central Europe and the heritage of the Austro-Hungarian Empire. The happenings inspired by the poets of the notoriously iconoclastic Bu-Ba-Bu triad, Yuri Andrukhovych (b. 1960), Viktor Neborak (b. 1961) and Oleksandr Irvanets (b. 1961), had their greatest successes in western Ukraine, especially in Lviv.[9] But the epicenter of Ukrainian postmodernism was the smaller western Ukrainian city of Ivano-Frankivsk.

Renamed in 1962 in honor of the eminent western Ukrainian writer and intellectual Ivan Franko (1856–1916), the city had been called Stanyslaviv until 1939, and then Stanislav. The cultural ferment associated with the city in the 1990s came to be called the Stanislav Phenomenon, a name that emphasized the movement's break with the immediate Soviet past and its intention to recover an earlier, Central European, cultural orientation. Not all the creative people associated with the Stanislav Phenomenon lived in Ivano-Frankivsk. Yuri Andrukhovych did so, but Yuri Izdryk was born in nearby Kalush and moved relatively early to Lviv. "Stanislav" became, rather, a symbolic point of coherence for writers and other artists of a certain generation (most were born in the 1960s) who shared an awareness of creating nontraditional work that responded to a global cultural context and drew inspiration as much from European literature and Western philosophy as it did from local experience and tradition. The movement's primary appeal was to the more adventurous part of the high culture elite, though it incorporated elements of popular culture, especially in its frequent moments of parody. Its emphasis was on literature, though its journals and almanacs can hardly be imagined independently of the remarkable graphic art that accompanied the poetry and prose on their pages. Volodymyr Yeshkiliev (b. 1965), who claimed credit for inventing the name "Stanislav Phenomenon" and dedicated considerable effort to mythologizing it, in part by describing it in words drawn from the vocabulary of poststructuralist criticism, had the following to say of it in the *Short Ukrainian Encyclopedia of Contemporary Literature* (1998):

> The phenomenon of the presence in the city of Ivano-Frankivsk...of a group of writers and artists whose works represented the most advanced expression of the values of...Ukrainian PM [postmodern] discourse. The creative and organizational activities of this group made possible several synthetic projects that opened up PM discourse in contemporary Ukrainian literature and brought its range of manifestations to a certain completeness. Central among these projects were and continue to be the conceptual journals *Chetver* [Thursday] and *Pleroma*, as well as Yuri Andrukhovych's editorial projects under the aegis of the

> journal *Pereval* [The Pass].... The historical context of the Stanislav Phenomenon was the disintegration of the USSR and the situation of cultural "openness" that rendered inevitable a change in aesthetic standards and artistic coordinates, as well a transition, not organic but abrupt, from a literature dominated by TR [testamentary and rustic] discourse to the global literary metagestalt of PM discourse.[10]

In addition to the figures already named, Yeshkiliev's encyclopedia singled out as members of the Stanislav Phenomenon the prose writer Taras Prokhasko (b. 1968) and the poets Halyna Petrosaniak (b. 1969), Maria Mykytsei (b. 1965) and Yaroslav Dovhan (b. 1956). But the person most intimately and most continuously attached to it was Yuri Izdryk. Indeed, one knowledgeable commentator dates the Stanislav Phenomenon as emerging "when the engineer from Kalush, Yuri Izdryk, created the almanac *Chetver*."[11]

Who, then, is Izdryk? For all the biographical notes published in printed sources, and despite the impressive array of reportage on and interviews with Izdryk on the web, it is not easy to penetrate to the facts of his biography or to separate reliable information from mystifications in the spirit of postmodern play. Ihor Bondar-Tereshchenko (b. 1964), a critic working in Kharkiv in eastern Ukraine and perhaps for that reason not *a priori* infatuated with the doings of the Ivano-Frankivsk coterie, once authored the not inapposite English-language pun, "Izdryk is trick."[12] "Trickiness" is indeed a quality of the autobiographical entry "Izdryk" in the famous third issue (1992) of *Chetver*, which was organized as a glossary of names and terms relevant to the contemporary Ukrainian nontraditional arts:[13]

> IZDRYK (De Ribas), Yurko—that's me. (See also "human being.") Sixtier by date of birth. Chemist by place of birth. Hygienist by conviction. Eternal dilettante. Worked in the fields of music, literature and the visual arts. Had no success in any of these but always showed promise. Character: a paradoxical combination of extroversion bordering upon exhibitionism and pathological introspectiveness. Mutant. Hero of the Battle of Chornobyl. A yearning for a synthetic art form prompted Izdryk to found a journal of texts and visions. Thus *Chetver* came into being. Anticipates several years of vain exertion and wars of liberation against surroundings.

> Regular mild depressions combine with irregular and imaginary catharses, yielding a satisfactory average. In 25 percent of cases early death from cancer is possible, but a long and happy life is also likely, amen.[14]

Less suggestive but more informative is the web site of Kalvariia, the publisher of Izdryk's more recent books:

> Born 16 August 1962 in Kalush, Ivano-Frankivsk oblast. Graduated from the Faculty of Mechanical Technology of the Lviv Polytechnic Institute...(1984). Worked for two years in the Ivano-Frankivsk automated metal casting machine plant, then in the Kalush Salt Research Institute (1986–90). Editor of the nonperiodical journal *Chetver* since 1990.[15]

In addition to literary texts, Izdryk was the author of a concerto for piano and two tape recorders and mounted at least two exhibitions of collages assembled from personal papers and objects. In interviews for the media he was often frank to the point of confessional intimacy, presenting himself as inclined to misanthropic sentiments and to the abuse of alcohol and narcotics.[16] Izdryk was no less open in dialogue with journalists about his belief that a religious framework is necessary for human action, remarking that "there is only one good fear: fear of the Lord."[17] In 2003, interviewed by Taras Prokhasko, he identified several writers who had once had significance for him: Erich Maria Remarque, Ernest Hemingway, Kobo Abe, Kenzaburo Oe, J. D. Salinger, Julio Cortázar, Max Frisch, Jorge Luis Borges, Samuel Beckett, Andrei Platonov, and Franz Kafka, but claimed that only Vladimir Nabokov continued to give him pleasure. He spoke favorably of Martin Heidegger and of the modern Ukrainian classics Vasyl Stefanyk and Olha Kobylianska.[18] Challenged to give an account of himself as a creative person, Izdryk identified *Chetver* as his main achievement and editing, rather than writing, as his vocation:

> I have sought various forms of self-expression—music, the visual arts, literature—and I suppose that there is some significance in the fact that I attached myself to literature in the end. But even here I positioned myself in the first instance as an editor and last of all as a writer. This way of being in literature—editing a journal—brings me the greatest pleasure. What is more, I think that's what I do best.[19]

While it is difficult to take at face value this accomplished verbal artist's indifference to his output as a writer, in some ways his prose does appear secondary to his other activities. At the time of this writing (2006), the body of Izdryk's work that had been granted the gravity of book publication was surprisingly small, comprising four slim volumes: *Votstsek* (Wozzeck, 1997), *Ostriv Krk ta inshi istoriï* (The Island of Krk and Other Stories, 1998), *Podviinyi Leon* (Double Leon, 2000), and *AM™* (2005). Much of the text that found its way into these books began life in the form of relatively autonomous journal publications. As for his most acclaimed work, *Wozzeck*, Izdryk resisted the idea that it justifies consideration as a serious literary achievement, insisting instead that it be understood as "autotherapy" or "autopsychotherapy."[20]

The two books following *Wozzeck* appeared with the same small publisher, Lileia-NV, in Ivano-Frankivsk. The cover designs, by Izdryk himself, were sufficiently similar to suggest that all three books should be treated as parts of a whole. No continuous story spanned the three parts, nor did the reader encounter the same characters in each, but there was a certain unity. All three focused on a fragile, anxious, threatened male, gripped by uncertainty as to whether the external world is reliably represented by the impressions that it makes upon his consciousness. All three shaped this theme using formal devices that, by the mid–1990s, were more than familiar as the stock-in-trade of literary postmodernism: parody, wordplay, quotation, allusion, montage, irony, paradox, amplification—the full toolkit needed to ward off any idea of a linear narrative, of a seriously held and readily communicated belief, or of coherent human character continuous in time. At the same time, the three books articulated a yearning for these very things.

In *The Island of Krk*, a collection containing narrative texts whose composition predated *Wozzeck*, the title story delved with characteristically Izdrykian intellectual and verbal flair into the theme of love. In *Double Leon* the narrative of a course of treatment for alcoholism became the pretext for complex language games. The prose shifted frequently into languages other than Ukrainian (Chinese in particular), and the book offered the reader a denser web of allusions to other literary and cultural contexts than was customary even for Izdryk. Here, perhaps even more poignantly than in *Wozzeck*, the negation of a unified personality was also the expression of a profound nostalgia for it. *AM™* was, in some respects, Izdryk's most masterly work, and in others his most appalling. Several at first seemingly autonomous tales revealed themselves, through the presence of motifs or events in more than one narrative, to be thoroughly (and artfully) interconnected. Yet readerly pleasure derived from the contemplation of this finely spun narrative web was counterbalanced by the grimness of sexual violence presented graphically and with black humor, but without the consolation of a moral framework such as might have been provided by satire.

Located at more or less equal distance from the sentimental utopianism of *The Island of Krk*, the extravagant mannerism of *Double Leon* and the decadent beauty-through-horror of *AM™*, but manifesting aspects of each, *Wozzeck* can still claim to be the text most representative of Izdryk's opus. It is also the text that houses Izdryk's most thought-through responses to the problem of aesthetic form in a world where there are no unchallengeable presuppositions and where the orthodoxies of poststructuralism grant credence to skepticism alone.

Izdryk's *Wozzeck* is the fourth in a somber dynasty. The first was a historical personage, the barber and former soldier Johann Christian Woyzeck, who murdered his lover out of jealousy in Leipzig in 1821. The second was a dramatic fragment, *Woyzeck*, written in the 1830s by Georg Büchner (1813–1836), a German writer, physician and radical intellectual. The work was based on the author's close acquaintance with the legal and medical literature concerning Woyzeck, whose case had attracted extensive public interest. Büchner's text, unpublished in his time, was lost until 1878; it was published in 1879 and performed in Munich in 1913.[21] In the following year the Austrian composer Alban Berg (1885–1935) began work on an opera, *Wozzeck*, that premiered in Berlin in 1925. Berg was a student and follower of Arnold Schoenberg, whose atonal music posed a radical challenge to the harmonic conventions of European art music. Atonality appeared to be an especially apposite vehicle for expressing the anguish and psychological distress of the central character but was so foreign to the conventional musical taste of the time that controversy and public anger attended the opera's Berlin premiere, while the Prague production of the following year was withdrawn from the repertoire in response to protests.[22]

Izdryk's *Wozzeck*, no less challenging in its formal composition to a traditionalist aesthetic sensibility than was its operatic predecessor, retains only a few markers of its indebtedness to the received Woyzeck-Wozzeck plot: the name of the main character, his condition of psychological distress, the importance of jealousy within his emotional repertoire, and the motif of the loss of the beloved (though not, as in the Büchner and Berg variants, as a result of her death at his hands). Like the other Wozzecks, Izdryk's central character perceives reality in unconventional ways, reflects on philosophical problems and proves to have at his command the conceptual instruments needed for such thought. At the same time, each of the Wozzecks speaks an eloquent and vivid vernacular idiom. Büchner's and Berg's express themselves in a German that is simple and strongly colored by dialect but richly metaphorical, while Izdryk's communicates in an intellectually sophisticated but fluent and vigorous Ukrainian that steers well clear of the scholasticism of some of the author's Ivano-Frankivsk colleagues.

Wozzeck was quickly recognized as an important text by critics attuned to the more experimental domains of Ukrainian literature. Already in the afterword to the first edition, Lidiia Stefanivska focused on the formulation in *Wozzeck* of a tension between the conception of the human being as thrust, tragically, into an indifferent or hostile world and a quest for redemption that is explicitly religious.[23] This tension, as I argued in the essay that was reprinted as the introduction to the second edition of *Wozzeck*, is superimposed upon the articulation of the methodological principle of radical doubt concerning every positive statement and every concept. One of the philosophical exercises that the text wittily presents to the reader is the demonstration of the slipperiness, indeed the unsustainability, of the concept of "self." The chapter "In Quest of the Person" contains, in the form of a parodied science-fiction narrative, the account of a journey inside the human brain in which the imaginary ever-diminishing traveler penetrates to ever deeper structures of matter, contemplating first the anatomy of the brain itself, then its cells, then molecules, atoms and subatomic particles. But the Grail of the quest, the "I," is nowhere to be located. The passage is a *tour-de-force* illustration of a deconstruction in the spirit of Jacques Derrida: a concept whose pragmatic validity we do not question in everyday life reveals itself, when teased and prodded and subjected to insistent questioning, to be contingent and insubstantial.[24] Svitlana Matviienko read *Wozzeck* as participating in a discussion that involves figures from the literary and intellectual canon both modern (Kafka, Nietzsche, Artaud, Mallarmé, D. H. Lawrence, Proust) and postmodern (Blanchot, Bataille, Deleuze, Guattari), as well as two eminences of Central European significance who lived in western Ukraine, Leopold von Sacher-Masoch and Bruno Schulz.[25] Izdryk's exploration of the psychology of desire captured the attention of Maryna Romanets.[26] Most commentators, especially Vasyl Kostiuk, Leonid Kosovych and Rostyslav Semkiv, had things to say about the text's formal qualities: its invocations of other texts; its parodic control over a wide range of styles and dictions; its puns and other acoustic wordplays; its skillful use of plot and character even as it explicitly describes its strategy to deny the possibility of either; and its capacity to generate readerly pleasure through its expert pretense at imitating the real and through its no less convincing renditions of the manifestly unreal.[27]

Most of the critics who offered interpretations of *Wozzeck* couched their readings in a tone of approval that was as much a tribute to Izdryk's text as it was a sign of their solidarity with the project of modernizing (or postmodernizing) the Ukrainian literary process.[28] But the significance of *Wozzeck* extends beyond the novel's contributions and challenges to a particular national literature. *Wozzeck* is a European philosophical novel that takes upon itself the task of deliberating over the possibilities of knowledge and belief on the one hand and moral action on the other. In its mockery of Descartes and Kant the novel takes skeptical cognizance of the Enlightenment tradition of understanding the subject as autonomous and rational, and consciousness as the ground of being. It parodies Heidegger: against his famously etymological emphasis on the connection between concepts and the primordial meanings of the words that carry them, *Wozzeck* pits the subversive Izdrykian ear for the ambiguities of words and the random and absurd connections that acoustic similarity creates between them. But *Wozzeck* does address the challenge, foregrounded by Heidegger and the existentialist tradition, of being-in-the-world and being-with-others: the novel's love plot is the formulation of a yearning for ways of being that might bring the "I" out of its tragic self-enclosure. *Wozzeck* enters into these discussions, fully alert to the radical doubt that the poststructuralist environment renders obligatory. Any precept or insight that the novel might offer can only be proposed together with qualifications as to its truth claims. In this spirit of tentativeness, of vacillation between affirmation and skepticism, the novel invokes the possibility of Christian belief. Both its chapters end with the Lord's Prayer, but lest Christian theism appear to be offered as the novel's "position," the text of the prayer is represented graphically as breaking into disconnected syllables and, finally, letters.

Wozzeck is an original and impassioned formulation of a tragic view of the contemporary predicament of the inheritors of the Christian and Enlightenment traditions. It is, for all that it is also a postmodern game, a reflection upon what it is to be of Europe, of the West, and of the modern world.

* * *

In the body of the translation, as well as the introduction and notes, the transliteration conventions of the Library of Congress system have been adjusted as follows: initial "ia," "iu" and "ie" appear as "ya," "yu" and "ye"; terminal "yi" is rendered as "y"; the soft sign is not transliterated; and the personal name "Iurii" is given as "Yuri," following a precedent established by recent English-language publications. In formal references to sources, however, the LC transliteration system has been used without modification.

I thank Myroslav Yurkevich for his careful and sensitive reading of this translation, and for his excellent suggestions.

Marko Pavlyshyn
Monash University, Melbourne

NOTES

[1] [Iurii] Izdryk, *Podviinyi Leon: Istoriia khvoroby* (Ivano-Frankivsk: Lileia-NV, 2000), 38.

[2] For accounts in English of developments in Ukrainian culture and literature in the 1980s and 1990s, see Solomea Pavlychko, "Facing Freedom: The New Ukrainian Literature," in Ed Hogan, ed., *From Three Worlds: New Ukrainian Writing* (Boston, Mass.: Zephyr, 1996), 11–18; Tamara Hundorova, "The Canon Reversed: New Ukrainian Literature of the 1990s," *Journal of Ukrainian Studies* 26, nos. 1–2 (2001): 249–70; Marko Pavlyshyn, "Demystifying High Culture? 'Young' Ukrainian Poetry and Prose in the 1990s," in Todd Patrick Armstrong, ed., *Perspectives in Modern Central and East European Literature: Quests for Identity* (London: Palgrave, 2001), 10–24; Marko Pavlyshyn, "Literary Politics vs. Literature: Ukrainian Debates in the 1990s," *Soviet and Post-Soviet Review* 28, nos. 1–2 (2001): 147–55; Vitaly Chernetsky, "The Trope of Displacement and Identity Construction in Post-Colonial Ukrainian Fiction," *Journal of Ukrainian Studies* 27, nos. 1–2 (2002): 215–32; Mark Andryczyk, "Bu-Ba-Bu: Poetry and Performance," *Journal of Ukrainian Studies* 27, nos. 1–2 (2002): 257–72; Maryna Romanets, "Ideologies of the Second Coming in the Ukrainian Postcolonial Playground," in Lisa Z. Sigel, ed., *International Exposure: Perspectives on Modern European Pornography, 1800–2000* (New Brunswick, N.J.: Rutgers University Press, 2005), 205–31; and Michael M. Naydan, "Ukrainian Literary Identity Today: The Legacy of the Bu-Ba-Bu Generation after the Orange Revolution," *World Literature Today* 79, nos. 3–4 (2005): 24–27.

[3] See Solomea Pavlychko, "Modernism vs. Populism in *Fin de Siècle* Ukrainian Literature: A Case of Gender Conflict," in Pamela Chester and Sibelan Forrester, eds., *Engendering Slavic Literatures* (Bloomington, Ind.: Indiana University Press, 1996), 83–103.

[4] For discussions of this polarity, see Mykola Riabchouk, "The Nativist-Westernizer Controversy in Ukraine: The End or the Beginning?" *Journal of Ukrainian Studies* 21, nos. 1–2 (1996): 27–54; Oleksandr Hrytsenko, "Culture as a Nation-Building

Tool in Contemporary Ukraine," *Journal of Ukrainian Studies* 26, nos. 1–2 (2001): 225–38; and the most extensive account of its literary manifestation in Ola Hnatiuk, "'Natywiści' kontra 'modernizatorzy': zmiany i stałe punkty w europejskiej debacie" ["Nativists" vs. "Modernizers": Change and Continuity in the Debate on Europe], chapter 3 of her book *Pożegnanie z imperium: Ukraińskie dyskusje o tożsamości* [Farewell to Empire: Ukrainian Discussions on Identity] (Lublin: Wydawnictwo Uniwersytetu Marii Curie-Skłodowskiej, 2003), 121–71.

[5] For a discussion of the tension between traditionalism and avant-gardism in Ukrainian literature of the 1980s and 1990s, see Marko Pavlyshyn, "Literary Canons and National Identities in Contemporary Ukraine," *Canadian-American Slavic Studies* 40, no. 1 (2006): 5–19.

[6] Volodymyr Yeshkiliev proposed a tongue-in-cheek tripartite classification of recent Ukrainian literary texts according to their adherence to one of three discursive types: NM (neomodern), PM (postmodern) and TR (testamentary and rustic). In the value system of the nontraditionalists, identification with NM and PM discourse conferred approval, while the TR label signified its opposite. Volodymyr Ieshkiliev, "NM-dyskurs," "PM-dyskurs u suchasnii ukraïns'kii literaturi" and "TR-Dyskurs," in Volodymyr Ieshkiliev and Iurii Andrukhovych, eds., *Mala ukraïns'ka entsyklopediia aktual'noï literatury* (Ivano-Frankivsk: Lileia-NV, 1998), 81–82, 91–92 and 108–9.

[7] Marko Pavlyshyn, "The New Obscurity: Adventures in Contemporary Ukrainian Literature," in Helmut Heinze and Christiane Weller, eds., *Die Lektüre der Welt/Worlds of Reading: Zur Theorie, Geschichte und Soziologie kultureller Praxis/On the Theory, History and Sociology of Cultural Practice. Festschrift für Walter Veit/ Festschrift for Walter Veit* (Frankfurt: Peter Lang, 2004), 445–51.

[8] For a detailed discussion, see Marko Pavlyshyn, "Post-Colonial Features in Contemporary Ukrainian Culture," *Australian Slavonic and East European Studies* 6, no. 2 (1992): 41–55.

[9] The high point of such interaction between representatives of alternative culture and the general public was the festival "Vyvykh–92" in Lviv, described in detail by Alexandra Hrycak

in her article, "The Coming of 'Chrysler Imperial': Ukrainian Youth and Rituals of Resistance," *Harvard Ukrainian Studies* 21 (1997): 63–91. See also Mark Andryczyk, "Four Bearings of West for the Lviv Bohema," in Sibelan Forrester, Magdalena J. Zaborowska and Elena Gapova, eds., *Over the Wall/After the Fall: Post-Communist Cultures through an East-West Gaze* (Bloomington, Ind.: Indiana University Press, 2004), 238–50.

[10] *Mala ukraïns'ka entsyklopediia aktual'noï literatury*, 102–3.

[11] Ihor Klekh, "Fenomen Stanislava," *Postup*, 1–7 February 2001, no. 18 (676) <http://postup.brama.com/010201/18_7_2.html>, accessed 29 August 2005.

[12] Ihor Bondar-Tereshchenko, "Double Trouble," introduction to [Iurii] Izdryk, *Podviinyi Leon*, 5–8, here 5.

[13] Members of the Stanislav Phenomenon were nothing if not ironically self-reflexive, generating a spate of parodic reference works about themselves. Yeshkiliev gleefully identified this habit as a medical condition, the "encyclopedic debility syndrome." Volodymyr Ieshkiliev, *Votstsekurhiia Bet: Komentari do "vnutrishn'oï entsyklopediï" romanu Izdryka "Votstsek"* (Ivano-Frankivsk: Unikornus, 1988), 8.

[14] *Chetver*, 1992, no. 1 (3): 63.

[15] "Iurko Izdryk — prozaik, eseist," *Kal'variia*, <http://www.calvaria.org/autor.php?aid=43>, accessed 18 April 2006.

[16] "Kollazhnykh del master" [Izdryk interviewed by Liubko Deresh], *Stolichnye novosti*, 18–24 May 2004, no. 18 (309) <http://www.cn.com.ua/N309/culture/personage/personage.html>, accessed 18 April 2006, and "Izdryk rezhet liudei" [Izdryk interviewed by Anatolii Ul'ianov], *Proza*, 22 April 2004 <http://www.proza.com.ua/peoples/izdryk_rezhet_ljudej_2161.shtml>, accessed 18 April 2006.

[17] "Kollazhnykh del master."

[18] Taras Prokhas'ko, ed., *Iurii Izdryk* (Ivano-Frankivsk: Lileia-NV, 2003), 12–14, 24, 30, 36.

[19] "Kollazhnykh del master."

[20] "Iurii Izdryk: Rozmovy pro literaturu, 'Chetver,' muzyku etc." [Izdryk interviewed by Kateryna Hichan], *e-motion*

knyhy, 27 September–3 October 2005, no. 29, <http://www.e-motion.com.ua/issue29/books/roof/Jur_j_zdrik1.html>, accessed 18 April 2006; "Kollazhnykh del master."

21 See Otto C. A. zur Nedden, "Nachwort," Georg Büchner, *Woyzeck: Ein Fragment/Leonce und Lena: Lustspiel* (Stuttgart: Philip Reclam, 1973), 62–64.

22 Mosco Carner, *Alban Berg: The Man and the Work* (London: Duckworth, 1975), 53–56.

23 Lidiia Stefanivs'ka, "Pisliamova," in [Iurii] Izdryk, *Votstsek* (Ivano-Frankivsk: Lileia-NV, 1997), 100–109.

24 Marko Pavlyshyn, "'Votstsek' Izdryka," *Suchasnist'*, 1998, no. 9: 101–13, rpt. as "Peredmova," in [Iurii] Izdryk [and Volodymyr Ieshkiliev], *Votstsek & Votstsekurhiia* (Lviv: Kal'variia, 2002), 7–30. See also Marko Pavlyshyn, "Choosing a Europe: Andrukhovych, Izdryk and the New Ukrainian Literature," *New Zealand Slavonic Papers*, 35 (2001): 37–48.

25 Svitlana Matviienko, "(U)movy stseny" [review article on the Russian translation of Michel Leiris's *L'Age d'Homme* and *Votstsek & Votstsekurhiia*], Krytyka 7, no. 12 (74) (2003): 29–32.

26 Maryna Romanets, "Erotic Assemblages: Field Research, Palimpsests, and What Lies Beneath," *Journal of Ukrainian Studies* 27, nos. 1–2 (2002): 273–85, here 278–81.

27 Vasyl' Kostiuk, "Fragment i pastysh," *Krytyka* 2, no. 2 (4) (1998): 30–11; Rostyslav Semkiv, "Ironiia nepokirnoï struktury," *Krytyka* 5, no. 5 (43) (2001): 28–30; Leonid Kosovych, "Postskrypt," in Izdryk, *Podviinyi Leon*, 176–78, here 176. See also the opening remarks about *Wozzeck* in Oleksandr Mykhed's review of *AM*^{TM}, "Povernennia boliu, abo pryvatnyi peresliduvach iz syndromom Liubans'koho," *Dzerkalo tyzhnia*, 5–11 November 2005, no. 43 (571) <http://www.zn.kiev.ua/ie/print/51688/> , accessed 16 April 2006.

28 Among those who felt no obligation to display such solidarity was Ihor Bohdan-Tereshchenko, who was pleased to dismiss both the "how" and the "why" of *Wozzeck*: "The technique of the 'palimpsest,' so highly praised by the authors of the comments on the back cover...consists of no more than the selection of

appropriate quotations.... As for that sacramental 'Why?,' Emil Cioran was right:... 'They should send writing paper into madhouses—tons of it per inmate. Then they could practice verbal regurgitation as therapy.'" Ihor Bondar-Tereshchenko, "Likuvannia slovovyverzhenniam," *Literaturna Ukraïna*, 2 April 1998, 5. See also his "Pravyla povedinky uvi sni: Pro odyn 'roman dlia literaturnykh hurmaniv,'" *Kur'ier Kryvbasu*, 1998, no. 10 (106): 162–65.

Dedicated to all those

whose texts show through the lines of this narrative,
transforming it into a palimpsest[1]

Chapter One

NIGHT

The Return of Pain

The pain returned at night. "Again," he thought angrily. "And again, and again, and again." He would have to bear it, again, until morning. And morning would be who knows when. When time lost its unambiguous dimensions he had got used to the uncertainty of waiting. If only he could get used to its absurdity. "Again and again and again," he repeated, again and again.

It was best to lie motionless, but after a while this, too, became unendurable. Worse, he felt that sooner or later he would have to get up to urinate. Sooner or later. Could something be sooner or later? "What if I get up now—will that be 'sooner' or 'later'?" He crawled out of bed, trying not to lift his head, and made for the toilet, bending double. Instead of the usual four steps he had to take eight. Each echoed with a new wave of pain. "Time to start exercising my right to wet my bed," he thought. "Again and again. How sweet that must be—slowly passing water any time you feel like it. At your convenience. Comfort even on critical days. Like the birds of the air. This right is the highest achievement of democracy. Use it."

He watched the warm stream spiral and disappear into the white bowl, and suddenly he knew that consciousness would trickle out of him with his urine. "That's it! That's it! The law of interconnected vessels." The conclusion was exciting. But his attempt to imagine his brain as linked to a global sewerage network failed, and he fainted.

Consciousness returned some time later—not "afterwards" and not "soon" and not in a few minutes, but after the elapse of an unknown quantity or length of this time of yours-and-ours, and he realized that he was kneeling, his head pressed against the toilet bowl. Not the best attitude for the prince of the universe. "Disgusting," he thought. "Simply disgusting! Returning like this every time. And this consciousness of yours-and-ours—always waking from sleep and emerging from nonexistence and coming out of nothing. Come on, let's turn around and go back. It's all back there, my beloved country, my home, my dacha, my garden plot, my license plate. O child, O sister mine, let's hence to lands where you and I shall never parted be.[2] There all is not. There even death is not. It's not far, it's somewhere here, just over the Carpathians. Happiness is not, pain is not, day and night are not. How about it?" But return seemed inevitable. And return meant only pain. Only pain now. Pain now substituted for the whole world. The whole world was pain. He listened and found that this was not pain at its best.

Categories of Pain

As a last resort there had always been classification. So far.

To be honest, he hadn't achieved much success there either. He knew many varieties of pain but had classified only three. At least three. Undoubtedly three. Three, of course. The first was concentrated somewhere in the superior frontal gyrus. It was highly localized, occupying scarcely a cubic centimetre of the brain, but the pinpoint certainty of the place added a fresh nuance to his agony. He felt he could grasp the aching part with his fingertips and pull it out of his head as you pull a splinter from your finger. But this was an illusion. The pain lurked somewhere close by, just under the bone, but was reliably defended by the skull. His fingers tore involuntarily at the skin on his forehead, trying in vain to get in. Then they scrambled like spiders for his eyes, aiming to enter the brain through the orbits and scratch just under or just over the eyebrows. Nothing extraordinary in that. Pain is not always pain, not always only pain, always not only pain, but also, to put it pompously, the quintessence of itching.

Nor was the second variety a pure clinical case, as the saying goes. Its beginning, at any rate, was highly unusual: the skin on his head suddenly felt too tight and began to pinch, as the foot is pinched by a shoe one size too small. This was not too annoying at first, but at night putting his head on a pillow was out of the question: the chafed cabbage stalk began to burn with fire. And this was not the worst of it. Being powerless to hide his face in his hands or to clasp them around his head (wondering why the Apostle of Truth and Knowledge fails to come)[3] was not the worst of it, either, for in the end any movement at all proved impossible. Clenching the jaws in despair, tensing the neck muscles even slightly, swallowing or even blinking were enough to tighten the vise another turn, and then another, and another, until the clear waters of enlightenment (or enlightened clarity) broke within the aching membrane.

Nonsense. A lexical jungle. Real immobility was required in only one case (the third), when the brain dried up inside, shrank until it was no larger than the kernel of a nut, and this nut, braided out of exposed nerve endings and suspended like the tongue of a bell on some single precarious fiber of the spinothalamic tract, beat against the burning walls of his skull—walls bristling with red-hot spikes of the finest Spanish steel and goads made from the most authentic of Mesopotamian thorns steeped in the most Russian of tsarist vodkas and the most Indian of curares. Immobility by itself was no help. He had to find that single pose, that sole angle, that one-and-only relationship between the inclination of the body and head and the placement of the limbs at which gravity, arterial pressure and the weak firmness of the spinothalamic cord achieved an unstable and almost unreal equilibrium, and the hateful kernel that was the brain froze in short-lived weightlessness between the paradise of curare and the paradise of fire. But—O agonizing delusion!—an incautious heartbeat was enough to dislodge the kernel and send it rolling, leaping with indecent glee, toward...well, toward you know what. Trying to recover the lost and priceless equilibrium you/he twitched instinctively, and the kernel, barely controlled by its tether, flew in another direction, and the aforementioned goads voluptuously penetrated and plunged into the brain's tender jellylike body. The worst of it was that with each new throb the pain became more caustic and acute, and yet the cursed crescendo never ended in unconsciousness. At any rate, he was never able consciously to go to the point of unconsciousness, for when he was halfway there, at some high and excruciating pitch of pain, a terrible nausea and exhaustion immobilized him and forced him to surrender completely to its sound, yielding to internal spasms and cramps that he struggled to control with the tattered remnants of his willpower until danger showed itself from another direction and his body began to go numb, starting with his fingertips and working up his arms and legs. The tingling advanced further and further, deeper and ever inward, eventually reaching the heart, approaching it so closely that he felt his heart muscles go numb, and this felled him suddenly to the ground, and after that it was impossible to distill out any single element, because the tolling in his head merged into a continuous extended din and clangor and the howl of sirens and the whine of approaching bombs and the shrieks of a woman torn open by childbirth, and his head beat against the floor, and his body thrashed about in convulsions, thawing, melting out of its deathly cold.

Classification was the only thing that consoled him in times of leisure and struggle. He was still on his knees and needed no experiments to imagine the thing that awaited him. He used to be able to predict at least its duration—two or three hours, even a day, but now he knew for certain that the flow of time could freeze, extending a moment into a year or decade. It was as if someone were taking pleasure in watching, in fantastically slow motion, a razor slice through the imaginary flesh of the apple of an eye. "And so, buddy: Attention! Right dress! Uniform number three: today you are the bell of the ball again. You're just a professional bellhop, that's who. Be more careful, buddy. More bright metallic tension. More crazy bloody screaming."

He summoned the strength to get up, pull up his trousers and flush the toilet. Then he stumbled over to the bed. The crescendo was just beginning. He knelt down and braced his forehead against the cold metal truss of the bed. "Come on," he said, "Come on, why don't you. I'll hear this orchestra out to the end. Come on!" he yelled with all his strength. His cracked lips scarcely moved.

He was, unless I am mistaken, a few months short of thirty-two, and his name was Wozzeck.[4] Lord, how sick I am of all this.

In Quest of the Person

Obviously, something here is not on the level. There is something not quite right, not to say not quite righteous, in the semiprofessional impertinence of these exercises in synonymy, in their skeptical rhythms and their rhetorical syntax. The very sound of certain words makes it hard to believe what they say. Possibly the name was uttered too soon, and perhaps it was wrong to put the name next to an irreverent address to God.

What is more, a whole series of misunderstandings will surely result from the ambiguous relationship between "I," "you" and "he." That is, between me, you and him. That is, between Wozzeck and Wozzeck Incorporated.

In your quest for your own "I," in your attempts to crystallize out this elusive substance (a prerequisite for any encounter between the first and second persons) you always come up against the purely technical limitations of internal optical magnification—that is, of good old neurophysiological blowup.

It was, after all, quite predictable and logical that, as you looked for the "I" in the depths of your skull cavity, your gaze, full of hope, should first have surveyed the whole of the brain, that unfamiliar and untouched planet, seemingly uninhabited and comfortless, whose immobile, even imperturbable surface gave no hint of turbulent processes inside. (The body with the mechanics of its muscles, the hydraulics of its heart and blood vessels, the twilight peristalsis of its various serpentine tubes and the childlike agility of its thinnest epithelia is usually thought of as the apotheosis of vitality, whereas the command post, the headquarters of all this complex machinery that one would imagine to be seething with tireless activity day and night creates the impression of absolute inertia, of complete listlessness, of moronic paralytic indifference. If, continuing with these forced anatomical and astronomical metaphors, we were to compare the brain to a planet, we would have to choose a planet that was gray, tedious and awkward—the moon, for example.) After roaming about its desert surface for a while and inspecting without much enthusiasm all these convolutions and hemispheres, these thalamuses and hypothalamuses, these hypophyses, etc., you began your descent into the dura mater and the arachnoid, ever deeper and downward. You sampled this tender soil at the most disparate points, and your analyses became increasingly painstaking, detailed and complete. At the stage where you could no longer do without lenses or microscopes, neurons, synapses, axons and dendrites hove into view, and later still—nuclei, cell membranes and mitochondria. Here life was in full swing, but the cursed "I" was nowhere to be seen. Stubbornly you advanced into the depths of matter, and soon you had before you strange molecules that you smashed to pieces with the determination of an infant getting to the guts of a new toy. Later still, armed no longer with optical instruments but with various bizarre contraptions—Wilson chambers, electron guns, Doppler accelerators and Foucault's pendulums[5]—you examined atoms and, once again, nuclei, then protons, electrons and neutrinos, you performed impossible three-particle operations (two nuclei and a muon) using Coulomb's law,[6] also two-particle and one-particle operations, but of course all this was wasted effort and vain hope, for somewhere past the last threshold you came up against the one great indivisible and nonexistent Nothing—the glittering likeness of pure energy that stood at the foundation of all things and all worlds and, finally, the whole Universe.

It was time to look around and ask, "But isn't this a mirage?"

The quest for the "I" retreated into the background. It became tiresome and uninteresting.

(Observation of the internal censor: "A graphite dot made by the sharpest of possible pencils is merely the sign of a true geometric point—a sign infinitely large relative to the point itself, which, as is well known, has no dimensions.")

But after a time the "I," gloating with malice, reminded you of itself.

After that you had to wait—for a long time, admittedly, but your patience was fittingly rewarded.

Abandoning your fruitless searches and the aforementioned journeys into the interior, you accustomed yourself to enclosing the "I" within the surface of your body. You came to terms with the idea that a liver enlarged by excessive drinking, or this arthritis-deformed finger with its chewed fingernail, or this wretched growth in the middle with the insolent habit of rising to its full stature, filling with blood and demanding satisfaction—that all these things were also "you." (Enter the second person.) You even accepted the elementary sophism that the "body surface" as a concept is completely relative. After all, the transition from you, certainly animate, to your immediate environment, uncertainly inanimate, is strangely imprecise, blurred and ghostly. These atrophied tips of fingernails, this dying hair, this hardened armor of callused skin—where is the seam, the limit, the boundary that would separate and protect you from non-you? Is it possible that even here nothing is discrete, and that your transformation, your gradual transition into the thin air that you have just inhaled, or into the solid rock that your knees press against, is as fluid and invisible as the mingling of water with water?

And so you had to discard as obsolete this habit of identifying yourself ("I," "you," "he") with your biological shell. Your illness gave you several enthralling yet agonizing experiences in the course of which, suspended at the edge of life, you felt that you were neither body, nor your accustomed self, nor a person, but a kind of pulsating substance that might be inside or outside you and could fit inside a poppy seed or expand to the dimensions of the room. At such times you were aware without discomfort or anxiety that part of you was the above-mentioned metal bed, the stool, painted white and with a hole in the middle, the light bulb and the electrical wiring (of which you were as naturally, easily and confidently conscious as previously you had been of the blood streaming in your veins), as well as the window, the floor, the ceiling, the walls, the toilet, and the tap—all this was you, and you were all of this.

The pulsation of this imaginary bubble, this new and sovereign "I" of yours, was in no way dependent on your will or subject to any regularity. Such uncertainty drained and exhausted you appallingly. For no sooner were "you" no larger than an apple (and no sooner had this apple rolled casually out of your skull) than you instantly swelled up enough to accommodate a good third of the terrestrial globe. A whole gamut of vanities, anguishes and pains beset you, for suddenly you began to know and feel:

how somewhere inside you tectonic fissures opened and oceans of boiling lava bubbled like so much recently ingested soup;

how gigantic flocks of hapless clouds swirled within you as cyclones and anticyclones, spilling rain and shedding lightning and thunder as they went;

how scorching winds blew away whole mountains of sand and carried them hundreds of kilometers east, to the shore.

And yet (or furthermore) such phenomena could be of any dimension, for just as distinctly you sensed:

how a school of shy fish swims softly in a tiny forest lake (or rather, you distinguished the movement of each fish in all possible schools of fish in all possible rivers, lakes, seas and reservoirs);

how a few steps from your bed, in the wardrobe, the caterpillar of a gray moth gnaws its way into the officer's cloth of your old coat (in fact, you saw the movement of each whisker of each insect in the whole expanse of the world within your domain);

and how, like a wretched sack, of no use to anyone,
in one of the apartments
of one of the buildings
in an average city
of a small country
on a modest continent
lies your emaciated anemic body.

End of the Quest

We shall begin again: "Obviously, something here is not on the level. There is something not quite right, not to say not quite righteous, in the semiprofessional impertinence of these exercises in synonymy, in their skeptical rhythms and their rhetorical syntax. The very sound of certain words makes it hard to believe what they say. Possibly the name was uttered too soon, and perhaps it was wrong to put the name next to an irreverent address to God." Perhaps. But the presence of a celestial God renders visible the terrestrial identity of all three—Him, You, Me—and therefore frees you of further quests. You may rise from your knees. You feel able to get up unassisted—to get up, it is true, only to lie down again a moment later, but to lie down deliberately, of your own volition, and to encounter the arrival of night like any normal person, stretched out on your bed.

(And yet, and also, and yet also the most important things, probably, are not these exercises in the art of the syllogism but the almost conscious joy that you feel as you confess your sins and gratefully receive your penance.

And the fact that you perceive, with almost conscious relief, each trial as a proof of your own sinfulness, for even this you cannot believe on your own.

And the consolation that he-you-I derive from crawling on the floor, from kneeling, from cramps and convulsions and screams.

For in this collective penance there is not a shade of the physiologism of Sacher-Masoch,[7] nor any trace of the provincial Drohobych complexes of a Schulz.[8] It is simply that here, in this remotest cranny of consciousness into which pain cannot at once penetrate, is the nesting place of the quiet joy of existence made conscious. Illness, with its opulent set of instruments and games, gives what nothing else can give: meaning.

Illness, with its opulent set of instruments and games, gave Wozzeck what nothing else could give: meaning. Expectation, struggle, suffering and exhaustion—this was his, Wozzeck's, work, and he could neither shed nor avoid it. It was his, inevitably and unavoidably his, and there was meaning in that. There is always meaning in suffering. If meaning exists at all, of course. However that may be, Wozzeck sensed that there was something real in his burden. The pain took away his freedom of action, of movement and of choice. During his fits Wozzeck had no control over himself, was unable to vary his feelings or his methods of self-protection, had no choices of behavior or of forms of reaction—and therefore, oho-ho, aha-ha, had no doubts either.

This was real life, this life was right, and it was righteous.

And, most importantly, it was very easy to live this way.

Pain took away his capacity to think, protecting the aforementioned quiet joy from unsought metamorphoses, from pleasure in his own suffering and from the temptation of that lowbrow messianism you feel each time the pain begins to abate and you come face to face with yourself, after all, being one's own messiah for oneself in particular means nothing but simply being this is the banal problem of self-identification just as it is after all the no less banal problem of faith for how can one distinguish the you from the I or the I from the you howsomehow to protect oneself assoonas the threat of the loss of the I arises asthe threat of death which as one might expect you await as deliverance asasas a potion not of this world but somehow it always happens that as soon assoon as you seehimcoming you knownot what to do).

Here He Comes

You see him coming. Your former classmate. Or the woman alcoholic from next door. They found her son dead a year ago in the entrance hall, and the whole building heaved a sigh of relief, he'd got everyone's back up so much, that little bastard with the crooked legs and the hopeless collection of chromosomes. So someone is coming. And if you are not walking the same path, or if you are walking a path that is not the same, you can always find at least a tree between you. And therefore you can move in such a way—at a certain speed, in a certain rhythm, at a certain angle—that the tree, he and you form a straight line. The tree, he, and you. First he, then the tree, and finally you. The mechanism of the solar eclipse: the earth hides in the shadow of the moon. You hide in the shadow of the tree. The closer you get, the more difficult this becomes, for the angle of the arc subtended by the tree diminishes. There is an increasing danger of catching sight of the other's face—and it might prove to be familiar; there is an increasing danger of revealing one's own face—and it might be noticed. From then on it will be marked. Movement at this stage must be precise. It takes more practice than merely not stepping on the black floor tiles or avoiding the cracks in the asphalt.

It is more difficult even than riding on a bus, for example, and pretending that you have not noticed an acquaintance (that selfsame classmate or alcoholic from next door who has lost all the distinguishing marks of gender and, like you, lives on the holy spirit of a full cup), I repeat: pretending that you have not noticed an acquaintance when your own face is marked and you yourself have long been identified. You must hold out for the duration of one stop, but you must do so with dignity, avoiding any hint of insincerity or rudeness. It's not so difficult. All you have to do is avoid turning away, and then, with a well-rehearsed air of spontaneity or even lightheartedness/preoccupation, direct your gaze between five and ten degrees to the right/left of the unfamiliar-familiar face of the acquaintance-classmate and stare at the pimply cheeks of some girl or other or an elect-the-best-mayor poster or a passengers-without-tickets-will-be-fined notice. Sometimes when you are in a good mood and feeling in shape, you take the risk of turning straight toward him—that sworn friend and best enemy of yours who can come upon you anywhere so easily, so effortlessly, and recognize you anywhere, even where trees offer no protection, even on the bus where the two of you almost press up against each other and you have no choice but, turning toward him, to ignore him, to look past him, beyond him and into the depths of something visible to you alone, into the window opposite, for example, where a child's finger is drawing curious designs on the sweaty glass.

And they never dared! They never dared speak up! You were the stronger!

Actually, there is nothing special about nonencounters with people—nothing deserving blame or self-praise. People quickly get used to your absence. It is easy to convince them that you are somebody else who looks like you. It is much more difficult, for example, to learn to sleep for more than twelve hours a day. Sometimes you manage, without cheating, to hold on for fourteen hours, but you should not abuse this skill, for whenever you do so insomnia begins to stalk you after a few days, and being alive, at night at that, becomes absolutely unbearable.

He hated insomnia.

The Dreams Begin

You hate in-somnia. You hate nights without sleep. You hate nights without dreams. The world of your dreams is intact, coherent and intelligible, you enjoy it even though its coherence and intelligibility recently landed you in prison (a prison set up in your old school; the building bore no resemblance to your old school, but you knew it to be your old school nevertheless), where after unrecorded events you ended up humiliated and rejected, and your place was next to the shit can, and to rehabilitate yourself you had to kill your opponent, and you did this in the only possible way, using some kind of musical instrument, probably a guitar. You beat it over the head of the gigantic overfed thug until the strings broke, the bridge flew off, the soundboard split, until splinters flew in all directions and finally nothing remained but the black fingerboard with a metal bolt at the end, and your opponent's head turned into a bloody porridge, you can still see it, regardless.

Regardless of the fact that one day the whole expanse of the universe shrank to the dimensions of a tight dark courtyard or passage with peeling walls, a low arch and a closed door at the end, where a feeling of dreadful entrapment and doom lay in wait for you and a handful of others like you, under the dull light of a street lamp—regardless even of this.

Regardless of the fact that in one of your dreams the fear of heights was so intense—and this fear was the dream's sole content—that any fall would have seemed a blessing. Any fall. But in that selfsame dream, standing at a great height, you cast a golden shadow. From your great height you cast a golden shadow upon the distant earth, and that shadow glittered with the gold of the sun drowning in water. It glittered like white gold.

In yet another dream you had at your disposal knowledge of the hellish content of the earth beneath the yellow wheatfields. Which gleamed like yellow gold. You knew that the earth beneath was not just earth, but earth as a crypt, a treasure chest, and your knowledge was the content of that earth.

The people in your dreams were not tied, absurdly, to their bodily membranes, and you could freely combine them, housing several persons in the one body or dividing one into many, shuffling, swapping, matching people to others' bodies or even to objects or things, for the essence of things had not been fixed once and for all and manifested itself in the primordial wealth of all its possible variants.

Places and cities were also pleasantly and easily exchanged.

Fragments of various cities were situated in one, and those cities were everywhere and nowhere; you could turn the corner of your ragged public housing block and St. Mark's Square in Venice would open before you, full of abominable, unsightly pigeons, and from here along a narrow, slightly altered Warsaw street—the Artists' Union gallery is there; it is in fact a dead end—you could get to the Lviv railway station, which, however, was situated in Stryi,[9] while Lviv itself, as was quite proper, lay far to the west but consisted of only one building or, more precisely, one apartment to which you had lost the key, something for which, inevitably, there would be retribution.

Dreams dispensed with the need for the customary collusion of dimensions, and you might, for example, on the occasion of a truce with your colleague (your classmate, perhaps) drink vodka with him without looking him in the eye because you scarcely reached the top of his boots, and all this could take place in that same Lviv-Stryi railway station whose underground passages led straight to the trains of the Kyiv metro.

You could be talking to a woman at a table in an open-air cafe and at the same time be the table, and the woman, and the cobble-paved square that was visible from the terrace, and the owner of the cafe, who was hosing down the cobblestones at the entrance to wash away the settled morning dust, and the dust itself or the water, and nothing else, because there was nothing else in that dream, the world consisted only of the items enumerated, and the enumerated items also comprised you.

In addition, taking advantage of the absence of fixed dimensions, you could love a woman not as a man customarily has no alternative but to love her, but, for example, as a human being loves a landscape (is there such a thing as the love of a human being for a landscape?), you could travel along her, you could live not with her but in her, you could, if you wished, take the pleasure of her body as a colony of viruses does, or a network of metastases, which, undermining the body from within, causes its death, death, death, my dear (gleaming with red gold)!

It is sad never to see anything but the surrounding reality, unintelligible and unchanging, and therefore even more unintelligible.

Dreams Continued

It is sad to know that you may not carry into this reality even a fragment of the eternal reality of the night, which, being intelligible, is mutable. So mutable that it is fleeting and ephemeral; it is a reality that in the light of day burns out, loses color and disappears before your very eyes, like those underground Roman frescoes.

In the morning you cannot for the life of you recollect the shape of the shadow of white gold that, terrified of the height, you had cast upon the distant earth below. But the shadow had a shape, undoubtedly it had a shape, divine and perfect, and this shape could have told you much of your own essence, for it is only through shadows that we may contemplate our selves.

In the morning you are unable even to imagine the pleasure that you brought a woman as you entered her, entered her entirely, wholly, to the full, walking at full height into caverns lustrous with the gleam of red gold.

In the morning you have no power over even the simplest images, as, for example, in the erotic episode from the dream about the yellow wheatfield and the mysterious content of the earth-as-crypt. A woman, her back turned to you—you could only guess at her face—was making breakfast in a kitchen that reminded you in some intangible way of Pepa's[10] kitchen in Lviv (you had been rereading Pepa's letters before going to bed).

Next time Pepa appeared in person, but because that night you were trying to break the fourteen-hour barrier the conversation with him resembled a rondo or variations or, say, the Goldberg Variations on a theme from a Chinese Chang rondo.[11] Because before meeting Pepa you had seen Marta wearing someone's surprisingly voluptuous body, you met in the rundown communal baths where paint peels from the walls, and the beautiful Marta, escorted by slaves, was surrounded by handmaidens soaping her arms, back, belly and thighs and rubbing them with sponges and coarse mittens, and you, surprised by the unexpected magnificence of her body, touched her breasts that were strangely firm, as if carved in stone, but unsurpassable in form, and you could already sense the Chinoiserie of the dream, though it would unfold fully later, when Marta would suddenly disappear together with her slaves, towels and coarse mittens, and in place of this hygienic profusion would come twilight, the evening sky, and fields. Such was the end of the film by a dwarf director who somehow resembled Sebastian Moro (evidently he was Chinese, quite likely the scion of an ancient dynasty, for as a rule signs of degeneration have deep roots).[12] He was shouting in an incomprehensible language and running in front of the camera, and with him, over dark green grass the color of pure chromium oxide, ran all the characters, actors, makeup artists, set painters and assistants. Being of normal height, they were constantly getting ahead of him, and the camera stubbornly recorded all that was taking place over their heads, trying at first to follow the flight of two dark birds that suddenly appeared in the picture and flew into the depths of the future screen, that is, into the distance, toward the horizon, there to be transformed into the two columns of a persistent windspout. The texture of those columns, translucent in the dull light of the setting sun, was something the cameraman was determined to capture. Later, when the sun's rays no longer illuminated the earth but were still reflected by the low clouds, the lens suddenly caught a pair of brightly colored kites—this was as good as any ploy carefully prearranged by a film director—and for a moment the magic of the short-lived and beautiful spectacle captivated the whole group. Almost everyone felt strangely uplifted and joyful, most of all the dwarf Chinese, who alone, perhaps, understood the meaning of what was happening and only now became convinced that the film would be good.

So dreams bestowed yet another liberty: from now on events did not have to match your mood. Just as the sensation of the Chinese Chang rondo appeared long before the kites (and this was the sole direct and incontrovertible proof of a connection to the land of the Yellow River, for even the nationality of the short director could have proved to be a later, daytime, construction), so all your feelings, whatever their intensity or key, could arise anywhere and at any time, without any obvious connection to a plot. From now on you could experience the joys of conviviality while wandering alone over a labyrinth of railway tracks, your happiness in no way abated by the smell of the overnight damp of the sleepers, or their rhythm, which refused to correspond to the rhythm of your steps, or the whistles of distant shunting locomotives. Or, again—and the number of variants was endless—you could experience an ethereal, almost heavenly serenity as you ran from a crazed murderer and then died under his knife (more precisely, his merciless knife, which repeatedly penetrated and tore at your flesh, carving it into small pieces and stabbing and cutting again and again even when there was no further need), while fear, infernal despair and inhuman agony appeared in a completely different dream during an act of random copulation in a not very clean hotel room.

Soon you realized that your fear, pain and despair belonged to none of the images described here. For a long time they found no attachment to the phantoms and mirages of your dreams, until one day you saw, with a certainty that acquired the finality of a verdict, a small, almost square room. In addition to a toilet in the corner next to the door it contained a filthy white stool, its seat slashed. Next to the barred window stood a bed with a wire mattress and legs that had once been chrome-plated and now for some reason were painted to look like the trunks of birch trees. In front of the bed, his forehead braced against its metal truss, knelt a man whose face you could not see, but whose name suddenly surfaced in your mind as an inscription, erased long ago, might come to light on a parchment. "W," "o," "c," "k." Double "z." "E." Wozzeck!

An Entomological Sketch

W, o, c, k, double z, e. Double-you o sea kay, lover of girls today. Zeck, cicada, zack. Cicadas on the Cyclades.[13] Ye-es. People are OK, God bless them. As for things—you can put up with them, too. But plants and animals are sometimes intolerable.[14] All those birds that start at dawn and rob the world of its chastity and silence—especially the desperate screams of the turtledove, especially the tedious cooing of the female and the sharp jarring shriek of the male announcing his approach to the nest. This, especially. Or the various creeping things that prevent my girlfriend from freely spreading her legs. Pagan girls love sex in the long grass, especially in summer.[15] But in summer the danger of various creeping things entering the body is especially acute. In bed it is quite another thing. In bed you don't get the shiny little black insects that hatch from under the ground in early spring, you don't get ants—red stinging ants, nor large forest ants, nor the miserable Egyptian ants that live in the bread box and build a whole ants' nest overnight, a whole world in a half-eaten bread roll, a whole Egyptian, believe me, son-of-a-bitch world in half a loaf of gray bread: tunnels, galleries, corridors, secret chambers and mausoleums, the works. You can see them for yourself as you cut slices off their world layer by layer and bury or embalm the beggars under a really thick layer of imported margarine, so the danger of their entering your body remains. Even here.

So what do you get in beds? Bedbugs. That's well known, well understood and natural. But rare. Except, let me say, in communal apartments or ancient third-class carriages where the hard wooden benches have taken their tenth layer of sticky never-drying lacquer paint, and the partitions are poison-blue or dark green and have some sort of ornament carved into them. As a child you loved running your finger along its capricious ridges, following the strange curves and bends that you now know were Oriental in character, verily, verily, I say unto you.

Or cockroaches, very often encountered in the hospital wards that in our country are all identical, and therefore in the white ex-army cupboards, and therefore under the gray skirting boards, and therefore on the pale blue walls, in the orifices of derelict electric wall sockets, in the control panels of fictitious urgent nurse-call systems and on the nurses themselves, under the windowsills, behind the central heating columns (linked by pipes that stretch under the whole city to the Regional Heating Center; in winter at least, black or green-and-black thaw lines and persistent little clouds of gray steam betray the location of these pipes, especially if you look down from a great height, say, from an enemy dirigible—quite often you had to imagine yourself a spy, a robber and daredevil, for somehow you had to justify, motivate and make use of your unique ability to trace the plan of the subterranean pipes from the Regional Heating Center—a dirigible, after all, is not some lousy jet or satellite but a dirigible, dammit, and that, devil take it, brings us to the year 1914 of evil memory, when your relatives were croaking at Ypres[16] of a stinking gas that newspaper hacks (loathsome creatures, not a shred of conscience among them) labeled "Yprite" the very next day while the iron, as they say, was still hot, and you feel nothing but loathing for the legions of red, almost black cockroaches that reside in all the places enumerated above, especially the hospitals, they are so numerous that even jars of water don't help—the jars of water into which, with much labor, you finally maneuver the legs of your bed in the hope of stopping insolent representatives of the ubiquitous creeping things from scrambling all over your body at night.

Dirigibles, on the other hand, are free of them.

Further south you get scolopendrae. You have to hit them with a steam iron as they crawl along the wall. The trail that the scolopendra leaves on the wall is aesthetically pleasing, unlike the scolopendra itself, which in children's books is still sometimes foolishly and indulgently called the centipede, what kind of damn centipede is it, I ask you, it's all worm and fish and snake, and with legs, too, hundreds of them, they are like ribs that poke out into the open, period. Things—they are OK, God bless them. Period. But as for everything else—no period

A Life by maupassant

One night I had a dream in my white room about a guy who was sick in the head. I was moved, he gave me hope at first, I got used to him, I began to like him and to think as he did, I tried to copy his illness, but it turned out that he, too, had dreams, and one day he dreamt me sitting at my desk, bent over in my sympathy for him. This prodigal and profligate circle is hard or even impossible to break. The main thing is not to skip ahead but to match the rhythm of the words to the rhyme of your steps, so before you get to Wozzeck's dreams you need to go through the dream about Wozzeck, and that won't be any time soon. What did happen soon was that you had a vision of Guy de Maupassant's *A Life*,[17] which made you think again about the freedoms that night bestows. Freedom from time, from the obligation to be both yourself and everyone, freedom from the inevitable coherence of events, from the fluid and the rigid, from surprise and recurrence, from the need for repetition and from the non-novel called *A Life* written by Maupassant, period.

But at the beginning, four dreams earlier, it was quite, quite different, I say unto you. For unto you came a poetess, one of those young poetesses who always hand you a folder of their poems before they hand you their body, bang-bang, that's how it was this time, too. You, not a very young poet, were visited by one of those young poetesses; you sat on the sofa, somehow elevated above everyone else (you did not know yet that this was a stage raised above an auditorium), you were reading from a thick tattered notebook, possibly aloud, in any case some passages were unclear, and when you asked about an illegible line your guest leaned over the notebook, but actually she leaned over your knees, she practically lay down on you, and here...and here the whole piece, this whole episode of your dream repeated itself, for it turned out that the way you sat on the sofa was awkward and inconvenient and would complicate your efforts to make the following events seem plausible, and your remark that from a distance you probably looked more like lovers than people reading poetry, this remark of yours sounded wrong, even though you knew your lines perfectly (so at that moment there was already a script, and the action was moving toward a predetermined finale!), and you did the episode again. This time you sat to the right of the girl and put the notebook on the sofa even further to the right, and you read out of the corner of your eye. Now she really did need to reach across and almost lie down in your lap, but this seemed so natural, the movement was so spontaneous, sincere and graceful that it would simply have been rude to object to this unexpected closeness of your bodies. The sentence in the notebook must really have been illegible, because the author herself could not make it out (or perhaps she didn't want to, you realized now), your knees were against her breasts, and her ear, such a pretty ear, ended up right in front of your lips, and then there was nothing you could do but whisper the phrase, memorized long ago, that from a distance the two of you probably didn't look at all like readers, and your likeness to lovers would become self-evident as soon as you touched her skin with your lips and then your tongue, and then lightly pressed her flesh between your teeth, begad.

There. And later it will become clear—as always, it will become clear all of a sudden—that you are playing not your own role, that is, not the role of a not-very-old poet, but of some teenager. You'll even become aware of this teenage self with a certain indifference. You won't be at all surprised. It will be as if all your life you had been fifteen—not you at fifteen, but some complete stranger. Then where does the young poetess fit in? And probably you won't be surprised when the father of this character of yours, this boy whose role you had to play and who had just screwed his girlfriend (although really she was your prize—the young poetess who yields to her confrere first her notebook and then her body), when, as I say, the father returns, you feel that you are the father as well, both of you, that is (nothing strange about that, all the characters in your dreams are always only yourself), and when you-the-father slip in a pool of seed cast carelessly upon the ground (how can this be known with such certainty about an event in the theater?), you-the-son will make an off-color joke, and finally the theatricality to which allusion has just been made will materialize and show itself to the fullest: the father will curse and hurl imprecations ("I don't want to see a trace of you here in the morning" is what was said, I think; it was getting late), the revolving stage will turn (this stage direction is entirely provisional, there being just a sofa on the stage), and a stage-set plywood ship will glide from the wings, symbolizing the morning departure of the expelled and accursed profligate son (you-the-son, who stole the prize from you-the-spirit and were punished by you-the-father). Taken together, all this will put you in mind not even of a farce but of a parody upon a farce, so what talk can there be of moral turpitude?

Well?

But what about Maupassant, Maupassant? Don't dismiss him in your irritation! After all, four dreams ago you dreamt not of Montpensier, not of a montagnard, not of Wes Montgomery on Montparnasse,[18] but of nothing less than Maupassant's *A Life*. The luxury edition stood where in reality you keep your moldy and unread volumes of Jules Verne and Jack London. A dark blue spine, gilt impressions and amethyst marbling along the edge. *A Life* was, for some reason, printed in volume two and not, as is usual, in volume four. Dense, perfectly smooth, stiff paper and illustrations, great God, what illustrations! O Heaven, Heaven, what magnificent, restrained, sunny pastel-and-watercolor hues! For some reason there was a picture of washing drying in the wind and sun. A multicolored sheet cast multicolored shadows on the ground, beautiful, truly beautiful, I say unto you, except that everything was reversed, as in a negative: the ground was dark green, a dull chromium oxide color, it was dark wherever there was no shadow, and where there was shadow it radiated, it simply flamed, it almost shone. Well, what can I say—such was the art nouveau or, put simply, moderne illustration on the page where Maupassant's *A Life* fell open.

But *A Life* was, so to speak, not quite *A Life*, because it contained a character from *Bel-Ami*,[19] an arrogant, brazen, dissolute fellow, just the partner for the fifteen-year-old captain of four dreams ago, but more experienced, naturally, more insolent and more mature. On one of the pages my eye caught the sentence, "That evening she allowed her knees to be fondled,"—did this expression really belong to the immortal Guy de? After that there were no more sentences, they simply could not break through the densely packed events of life. The desperate scum was trying to sodomize the heroine, if by sodomy is meant no more than a particular perversion, and, as if that were not enough, this was taking place under the influence of hashish, they were smoking hashish (I don't really know whether you smoke hashish or take it in some other way), and that brutal thug from Maupassant's novel was quoting the example of a female character in that same novel, he was talking about Roksolana, the supposed model of such unseemly behavior, who entered history because after hashish she could not engage in the above-mentioned kind of intercourse because the narcotic made a particular muscle contract. Today medical science calls this the "Roksolana complex."[20] That is what our dear friend was telling his dear friend as he approached her from behind ("let's see if your muscle has contracted, sweetheart"), and all this was under the influence of hashish, so without a doubt this was the epoch of permissiveness and sexual rebellion, when long-haired girl students, the free spirit of Europe, were going to revolutionize something or other, who can remember today what that was; when long-haired fifteen-year-old captains—the free spirit of Europe—sought nirvana in the overwrought tones of an Orient-orientated melos, when long-haired intellectuals—the free spirit of Europe—invigorated their intellectual libidos and the libidos of their Cambridge graduates with the innocent smoke of an innocent weed; when long-haired sweaty pilgrims—the free spirit of Europe—pursued happiness at crowded stadiums to the sounds of Hotel California, what am I saying, Hotel California came much later,[21] and the free, free, indestructible free spirit of Europe... (the sentence is incomplete). That said, your being and living inside the hide of a French miscreant should not surprise you, all the more so as, like the preceding sentence, this being-and-living has proved incomplete. The morning cut off your adventures, and the second volume in the dark blue covers never found its way back to its place on the shelves where in reality the unread Jack and Jules molder and smolder.

Here Come the Heroes

The air is thick with names, and now, on the eve of the great flood, the time is ripe for genealogy. A genealogy is a song in which names cannot contain their destiny and run like honey, like pitch, like cotton candy in children's sticky, dirty hands. Even names as exotic and as dear as A.

Here comes Miriam. I gladly overlook her face but cannot overlook the dirt under her fingernails or her missing fourth and decaying third upper (right) teeth. (These latter are independently visible, like the smile of the Cheshire cat.) Miriam is the only person whose coming doesn't irk me. Miriam's fingernails curve in all three dimensions, and if she didn't cut them they would curl themselves into hooks. That's why she cuts them short. But she doesn't do it often. She scrapes the dirt from under them even less often. Miriam's shoes repeat exactly the form of her toes, as in Magritte.[22] Magritte is a character from a satirical epic of Homer's. He thinks highly of his intellectual prowess, but he's a fool and a boor.

Here comes Nestor. Miriam can't stand Nestor. He is wet and limp, like jelly. He hugs and kisses me, and the jelly runs all over my body. A kiss from him and you are left with a mark that afterwards you cannot remove, no matter how long and hard you try. Marvellous.

Here comes Gorwitz. He says a quiet and reserved "hello," trying to hide the blazing energy that is consuming his guts. (Gorwitz is over forty, but he has more adrenalin than he can handle.) Before extending his hand, he wipes it discreetly against his trousers.

Here comes Ollie (Nigel).[23] He is bright-eyed and in love, and if you don't acknowledge his gaze he begins to suffer. Even before reaching the door he puts in so much suffering that I get pangs of conscience. So I try not to offend him, and with this slightest of encouragements Ollie (Nigel) blossoms into a smile beyond all words. He simply radiates. His third upper right tooth is rotten, too.

Here comes Miriam. With enormous effort she restrains herself for exactly two minutes, then bursts into gusts of raucous laughter, and all attempts to calm her are in vain. Miriam swells like a balloon and occupies the whole room. She vibrates, quivers, shrieks, hops about, and simply does not notice that you have long been cringing in a chair, covering your eyes and ears and trying fruitlessly to wall yourself off from the glitter of her gold and the gurgle of her tubes.

Here comes Karp Liubansky.[24] Or rather, he more than comes, he manifests himself. He throws you a pampered palm and a firm handshake. This is supposed to signify real masculine friendship. Or maybe solidarity. Usually you are glad to see him, usually he has a morning freshness, even if it is full of hints at last night's crumpled bed linen. Karp Liubansky expresses goodwill and respect and even simulates patronage, but at a convenient moment he slips away from you (me) with relief.

Here comes Putsyk. His thin moustache conceals a short lip, like that of a princess. Mostly he keeps quiet. Why he comes nobody knows. I secretly pick my nose. He does, too, I think. We part amicably. "His smile is pure gold."

Here comes Joachim (Yukhan),[25] a delicate, sophisticated youth. His speech is soft and ingratiating. He's an intellectual. It's hard to look him in the eye because he is cross-eyed. I don't catch his words, but I see his shadow behind him swell and loom over me, menacing and lascivious—there's a shot like that in the movies somewhere. Suddenly the shadow lurches off to the side and disappears, and Joachim (Yukhan) is left without one.

Here comes Miriam. She speaks heatedly about some book or other. Then she asks, why can't I (she) come with my own husband? As if I (I) knew. Try spit, I say. Or maybe I don't say it, just think it. It makes no sense to say anything.

Here comes Matiash Kudusai.[26] You (I) have loved him for so long that you don't recognize this as love. Kudusai is bewildered by your indifference, which you camouflage as fatigue, he is bewildered by your fatigue, which you camouflage-as-indifference-in-order-to-seem-to-love, he is bewildered by your love, which is not at all like his, Matiash Kudusai's, love for America. You (I) bid him farewell in a way that makes him feel guilty.

Here comes Schwarzkopf. He carries his belly as women carry large breasts—high, and with dignity. Over his belly he has spread his shaggy beard, peppered with dandruff. Schwarzkopf is remarkably sensitive and well-mannered. Responsible to the point of punctiliousness, punctual to the point of pedantry. He is delicate. Perhaps a little too nervous. Easily offended. Reads a great deal. Thinks even more. When he is sad, he is like me. His sense of humor is quick and precise, like an aquarium fish. The Gippius,[27] or whatever you call it. His philosophy owes more to emotion than to reason. Listens to the radio. Selective in the company he keeps. The only problem is, he has purple heels.

Here comes Miriam. She talks about this and that, biting her lip. She says good-bye. A minute later she comes back, and you have to take her right there, in the corridor. As you lick the salt off her spine, you are aware of a pervasive smell of urine.

Here comes Yakovyna. He kicks the door open. Or perhaps I exaggerate. He announces something the moment he enters. His jokes are frequent and mostly stupid. He's the only one who laughs at them. His laughter suggests a refined, complex-riddled personality and a complicated psyche. He likes to stay for ages, ignoring my eloquent hints. If I withdraw from the conversation, he sits in silence, reading old newspapers. He smokes my Brazilian cigars. The cigars are expensive, they're meant for important guests, but Yakovyna smokes them one after the other. I open the doors and windows and go out for a walk. When I return, he's still there.

Here comes Caesar. He extends his dead hand. He either says nothing or mumbles unintelligibly. Smokes stinking tobacco. If you do not talk to him about himself, he goes away. He is placid.

Here comes Borovchak. Waving his limbs. Giggling. Telling the latest stories as if they were the *latest* stories. Jumps from topic to topic. Giggles again. Folds his hands into a bread roll. Argues with himself and disappears in the heat of debate.

The lumberjack brothers arrive. Gustav and Gustav. There are three of them. Very noisy, too. Waving their axes. One is a schizophrenic, one a cupid, and the third is the youngest. Actually, they are the nicest guys of the whole lot because they don't give a shit about me, and I don't give a shit about them.

Here comes Miriam. She makes herself comfortable on the table, throws one leg over the other and smokes. She comes seldom, but at least she comes—for whatever reason. This Miriam, it appears, has straight white teeth. It's just her jaw that's crooked. I see only her glasses, her wavy black hair and the sharp little nose of a young witch.

Here comes Miriam. She has nothing on under her light dress. I'm bored as I take her, kneeling as if in church. Impaled upon me, she comes turbulently, and the stream of acrid odors that passes from her with her convulsions is punishment for my boredom and blasphemy.

Here comes Miriam. She sits down on the chair, spreads her legs like a peasant and rests her heavy breasts on her knees. She squints through her glasses. She asks with pleasant directness, "Well, what are you up to?" Indeed, what the devil do I get up to every day at this desk, in front of this clean sheet of paper and this perfectly sharpened pencil? Maybe I kill little girls. I run them through with this unbreakable Koh-i-Noor pencil,[28] I cut off their breasts, smash their teeth, gnaw through their neck vertebrae and stamp long and lasciviously on their glasses. I delight in torturing little boys. I stuff their gullets with clean sheets of paper of handy formats. I dismember corpses and hoard them under the filing cabinet. I mop up the stains with blotting paper and strew the floor with salt. I destroy all comers.

Here comes Miriam.

Only A. does not come.

Not ever.

Genealogy (Here They Come Again)

By inertia you hold in contempt old photographs and family relics and various talismans and gypsy ornaments, for all ornaments are pagan, you are annoyed by garments that conceal instead of shielding, you have no faith in people who tell beads.

As for the genealogy, we shall begin with Adenauer,[29] the only luminary who remained after Heidegger's ignominious flight. Adenauer, our infinite father, universal and multilingual, emerged from the dark unknown and disappeared into the darkness, leaving us his descendants and the melody of his name: "Add... 'er... now..."

Chateaubriand.[30] Then the Cyclops,[31] who appeared unnamed and unsummoned in his officer's boots at the Lviv-Stryi railway station and will do so again, in accordance with the prophets.

Waiting her turn after him is Marta, regally sad and lonely,

and behind her lurks Salvadoro Moro, the miserable Salvadoro of the house of Lao Tse and the Chang rondo, the famous director of underground films (error: Moro is called Sebastian).

After him you want to see Godot[32] next to Pepa,

but I'm afraid that Pepa, with his love for the Toronto Chinatown

("With the Chinese chicks it's great, mate, you just give a Chinese chick a compliment about her breasts, and she's yours. But I never had any luck with a Black lady."

"What do you say to them, the Chinese chicks? In the morning, I mean."

"Nothing much. They know about as much of the language as you do, so it's just have a shower and then bye-bye")

and his old-fashioned Lviv obsession with hygienics doesn't belong in the epoch of Marquet's boats,[33] syphilitic flies, servants, cold cream, and vervain.

So let him stand there by himself, dear old Pepa, free of hierarchies and regalia—who if not he could believe so passionately in Adenauer's forefatherhood? Pepa, Pepa, Pepa.

After that, a mixture of gray and gold: the miserable Bruno, the greenish Sacher, the gelatinous Nestor, the full-blooded Masoch, and the battle-ready and childless Weill.

Weill begat Karp Liubansky, Karp Liubansky interrupted Matiash Kudusai, Kudusai fell in love with Ollie.

O Nigel, moth of my agony! You appeared as angels of penance appear in dreams, you bestowed forgiveness and parting, and as I confessed, sinner that I am, with my reflection in your blue eyes, you took all I had. You took what remained to me. My loves turned to follow you. On this earth I was the haven of last resort for a few doomed and beauteous ones, but you appeared, O Nigel, you lowly moth of my fall, and the multitude kissed your footsteps, it followed you, vanished after you, and the horizon came up like a knife.

Such was Nigel (Ollie). He moved silently in Nijinsky's ballet shoes and someone else's gymnastics leotard, son of a bloated Irishwoman, he listened of nights at our keyholes, the villain, faithful spouse of the ancient Edda Miriam, he told fortunes at our door, threw mirrors down the stairs and strewed salt and chalk, poured honey, carved graffiti and, as ever, dissolved silently in the gloom like the prince of darkness, but in truth he was an emissary of light, though of a strange deity unfamiliar to me.

But God is One! Come to your senses!

Nigel begat two sons, and neither had progeny.

But Marta, the regal and god-equal Marta invoked by us at the very beginning of these annals, conceived a child by her own court jester, the dwarf Sebastian, and secretly miscarried, aborting a premature monster, nameless, noseless and lipless (with a harelip, that is), who, however, sidestepped the canonical genealogy and managed to pour his blood and sperm into the astral river of royal blood and sperm, thus delivering from mortality the immortal tribe of Adenauer; his harelip suddenly reappeared generations later in the son of quite decent people, a certain Putsyk, an unassuming and simple man, yet rather frisky and, like his distant ancestor, the honorable and revered Bastar, partial to women, especially women rural and unattached.

One of them, admittedly not rural but certainly unattached, a bored female, a little witch with a head of curly black hair and thick black growths under her armpits, delicate black downy hair on her buttocks, black but not delicate hair down her unshaven shins and between her legs surprisingly red and perhaps for that reason shaved bristles, could not avoid seducing—casually, for lack of a better pastime—our countryman, the frisky Putsyk. If only because he was Putsyk, if only to taste his harelip upon her so multifarious, so variform, so relentlessly animal lips.

And here, as quite often happens contrary to all expectations, there came into being a tight-knit, strong and faithful marriage, and the result of this marriage, this love (as I put it without hesitation), was a daughter, Miriam, so sweet, so clever, so promising. While still at school she began to write uncannily good verse and handled the other sciences quite well, too, even the exactest ones, she was pleasant to behold—no beauty, you understand, but pretty, her magnificent hair she inherited from her mother, ditto her extensive eyebrows, dark eyes, etc., and nothing boded ill until on the eve of puberty the girl was visited by some weird hormonal disaster, some uncontrollable explosion in her delicate organism, and—

her nails curled themselves into hooks,

her head grew disproportionately large, her teeth decayed,

the skin on her face turned blue, purple, pink,

and covered itself in blackheads, pimples and scabs,

and the once full-bodied curls fell out and lost their color,

and there remained only reddish tufts upon the swollen skull,

while unwanted hair appeared around the nipples

that never managed to develop into breasts brimming with cordial,

and her legs and feet remained short and small,

acquiring only the capacity to transform shoes into exact copies of themselves, as subsequently portrayed upon an ugly canvas by a dutiful pupil of Magritte's.

One should be fair and give this youthful Miriam her due. She neither gave up nor let herself go nor downed colors nor laid hands on herself. One might hold against her only her excessive use of alcohol, but who of us is without sin? She continued to write quite good poetry and, after an initial polyandrous frenzy, settled her choice upon a completely decent and quite good man (somebody else's husband, admittedly), with whom she lived, without offense to his wife and children, the rest of her burlesque and tumultuous days.

As we know, she bore him no offspring, so how the tribe of Adenauer survived is an absolute mystery, and yet survive it did, for how else can we account for:

Yukhan the Cross-eyed,

Borovchak Afflicted with Madness and

Gorwitz With always damp hands and

Caesar of Eternal youth with his eternally dead hands and

the three Immortal Gustavs and

Schwarzkopf the Hero of purple heels and

Miriam Why-can't-I-come-with-my-own-husband and

Miriam the Blessed-Virgin-of-the-salty-back and

Miriam the Golden-throat and

Yakovyna son of his parents, that straightforward chap

Yakovyna Esquire—that is to say, all of our heroes. Including, after all, that Wozzeck, Wozzeck That, your blundering favorite, the lickspittle, your dearest, the flatterer, the golden boy, the pest, the traitor, the protégé, though perhaps we should pay less attention to him than to A.—this name is so foreign and unusual for the voice and ear of your eastern Wozzeckian tongue—for not even the genealogy in itself, but rather the fact of the presence of these two in Adenauer's line prophesies great opportunities for your self-repudiation, dearest I.

Apologia as Canon

Ask for fear.

I beg you, ask for fear.

Ask not for happiness nor good fortune, for happiness and good fortune are ephemeral, and only the fear of temporality can soften the blows of misfortune and despair that come without fail.

Ask not for misfortune nor despair, but ask for fear, so that you may not be tempted by your own sufferings to rejoice in the luxury of humiliation.

Ask not for wealth nor pleasures, but ask for fear, for wealth manacles freedom, pleasures bring ruin, and only fear gives hope.

Ask not for peace, nor freedom, nor hope, for peace is the essence of pride, and freedom the absence of wanting and being wanted, and only fear is faith and contrition.

Pray not for faith nor atonement, for you understand not the meaning of these words, and fear alone, which you know since birth, gives meaning to all.

Ask not for all and ask not for nothing. But the above-named. Remember that the war lasts ***for all*** (Galician colloquialism[34] meaning "always," "constantly").

The war has been since the beginning of time and will be until time's end, that is, forever. Every instant sees the death of two people, one of old age and illness, the other of wounds, and thus the chain of death is unbreakable. And every instant two are born, one a child of humankind, the other—one knows not whose child, and so the comings of the beast will be as many as the exegeses of his number.

A kiss is an attempt to extend the esophagus.

Ask not for knowledge, ask not for love, ask not for death. Hark, sweetest, pray for fear!

And I shall give it thee.

And I shall be repaid.

You die in every paring of fingernails, in every shaking off of dandruff, in every hair lost in combing. What more do you need? You leave behind piles of excrement and streams of urine and sweat. All this is dead. What else do you desire? Ask for fear, dear heart. Fear will bring you alive and rid you of the fear of life.

There is nothing that you can ever take for yourself. You are not even sure whether you have hands or teeth. And all that you have he has given you, so learn at least to desire it. There will be as much of everything as there will be discourses upon his cross. So ask for fear, ask for fear, ask for fear, I entreat you.

Climb upon the roof, from your breast bring forth your last proud cry of terror and despair and climb back down. Step cautiously rung by rung down the rotting ladder, and from the third rung jump down, parting the front of the fur coat that you have thrown over your naked body, and be the holy fool no longer. Lie down beside the wall of your building and hide your face in your palms. Try asking again. If you fail, live on.

Beloved, ask not for consolation, hatred or inspiration. Create no worlds of your own. Betray me not with my friends, bestow not your loyalty upon me, and let us ***not*** be afraid together. Fear alone requires solitude, for it is the thing that in solitude one most fears.

Entering your body is the same as immersing yourself in snow, in water, in earth, in leaves. I fear this immersion as much as I desire it. Under the leaves there are worms, flowers grow under the snow, giant fishes lurk in the waters, but there is nothing beneath the earth. Damn it, what use are you to me, my beloved? When I talk to you, do you truly, undeniably exist? Fly away, fly away, fly away, I beg you.

The thermometer shows the temperature of my body. There is, therefore, a certain connection between this slender column of liquid metal soldered into a glass capillary and myself. The atoms of my body move energetically and bump into the atoms of the glass, and those into the atoms of mercury, causing it, the mercury, to increase its volume—is this not folly? Fly away, fly away.

I fear this quicksilver. I do not know the reasons for its movement. It would be simplest to break open a dozen glass flasks and pour their contents into one's insides where one would experience the temperature directly, but this, if one believes the books, would cause the temperature irresistibly to fall until it equaled the temperature of the surroundings—is this not folly? Fly away.

And, flying away, be silent. I shall ask for fear—enough of it for everyone, my dear Miriam, my beloved A.

Unless I am too afraid to ask.

Postscript:

What is the difference between a human being blowing a bubble out of bubble gum and one who is not? No difference. You want to punch both of them in the face.

Grand Hotel

Next (word crossed out) you found yourself in the Grand Hotel. You did not know as yet whether it was morning or evening, and you certainly had no idea that this was the Grand Hotel. You simply walked out of your by no means luxurious suite—truth to tell, it was a simple cheap little room with imitation oak walls and no amenities whatsoever, and it had been allocated to you and another traveler, as always happens, after long negotiations, mutual winks and nods and cunning manipulations involving banknotes of various denominations—you walked out in your house clothes, your towel around your neck and a bar of soap in your hand, you walked out to look for the bathroom, which in premises of this kind is usually located, for some reason, at the end of the corridor, and suddenly you discovered that there was no corridor in the usual meaning of the word, for outside the short and narrow antechamber there suddenly opened out a remarkable panorama of broad staircases, balustrades, terraces and galleries leading away in all imaginable directions and in all possible dimensions and at the most unexpected angles, stone tiles, spherical vaults, frescoes and pavements, weird beasts guarding cast-iron lampposts, and the lampposts themselves with their white dusty globes, their light dull as if put to sleep, and people as well, a mixed and variegated crowd that shambled about this way and that and hither and thither and wherever.

Somewhere on the lower floors there was music.

You stubbornly continued your quest for the bathroom (a sure sign of an early-morning dream), though it was unlikely that one could be concealed behind any of these enormous double doors of real oak, with their smoothly polished copper handles. Passersby wondered at your unkempt appearance, or paid no attention to you, or disappeared altogether for long periods, and then you meandered through the empty halls, inspecting the ornaments on the floor, not daring to peer into any of the rooms or make inquiries, guided rather by smell than by geometry, intuition rather than sound. In the end you came upon the bathroom after all. Its door was open, notwithstanding massive cylindrical counterweights, and the smell was unmistakable, but as the sign indicated this to be a women's facility you had no alternative but to assume the majestic structure to be symmetrical (an assumption not altogether implausible) and set forth in quest of a similar room (this time for men) on the opposite side of the imaginary axis of this imagined symmetry.

As you walked the evening grew more advanced, or rather the prevailing temporal indeterminacy yielded to a sense of evening, and when after several unsuccessful attempts to grasp the logic of this ancient edifice and several unintentional and as-if-enchanted returns to the stinking girls' room—open, but forbidden of access—you resolved to descend one floor in the hope, etc., when you, and when...in short, the guests of the hotel, who had made their appearance again, thronged and crowded past you in evening dress—dark dresses with plunging necklines and sparkling jewelry, lacquered shoes, tails, dinner suits, bow ties—what else could one wish for?

Evening, evening, indubitable evening reigned in these grim spaces!

You came across ever more crystal chandeliers, ever more people, and with them—smells, and lights (the place you needed continued to elude you), stairs thrown this way and that seemed ever more confused, carpets ever more worn; yet ever cleaner were the white globes adorning the heads of the phantasmagorical dogs (black, cast in iron, malnourished) with women's breasts and fowls' claws; yet ever more translucent and delicate was the cold marble of the balustrades, in which the cracks of old age and the delicate veins of girlhood entwined themselves into a network of unparalleled beauty; yet ever more eloquent were the frescoes, full of those selfsame fowls' breasts and hags' claws, but this time in combination with angelic faces, ribbons and pale blue wings; yet ever louder was the music, ever more pungent the aromas, ever more powerful the desires. You descended further and further still, until around one of the corners you espied the landscape of the lower hall, filled to the brim and even overflowing with people sitting, standing, even lying between columns, on pedestals and podiums, steps, skirting boards and parapets. Somewhere in the depths of the room an orchestra played amidst the green of a small orangery, there was dancing, waiters wheeled trolleys of food and drink, costumes distinguished by their elegance glittered in the distance, while nearby a long queue with bags and suitcases snaked toward the administrator's window, cutting through the throng of dancers here and there and dividing it into islands. Chaotic traffic raged in the center, all the way from the glass doors attended by liveried doormen to the broad stone steps that led to the elevators and the first floor and God knows where else. Closer to me a whole crowd of people set themselves up as if in the waiting room of a railway station. They laid out their things and cordoned off little domains. Some slept, others ate or played with their children, others still—like the couple of youths with shaved heads who had made themselves comfortable on the massive base of a Doric column straight underneath me—played chess. For some reason I was not surprised, although these swarthy, vaguely Asian types (Eastern or Southern) who sell stiff starched carnations at our bazaars, and also trade in narcotics and stolen cars, and also spread exotic diseases, and also commit rape and murder in the interests of their own sub- and infrastructures and their survival and expansion, as a rule prefer Mah-Jongg or, even worse, set up games of preference, whereas here there was chess (which in itself meant nothing at all, merely referring us to traditions more ancient than those, say, of Dagestan or Kurdistan—to cultures and even worlds that had been resolutely forgotten and concerning which little could be revealed by grids superimposed on square, circular or cruciform fields—while warning us of a threat much more serious, for example, than that of accidental death by a Chechen knife or even of strange tortures by Iskanderian enthusiasts.[35] This threat, too, was ancient and forgotten, and in it one glimpsed the face of the devil, real and not yet vulgarized by the feeble European imagination), and yet, for some reason, as I said prev-

Chessmen

iously, I was not surprised but climbed over the terrace balustrade and was about to jump down onto the only free space that could be seen (it was next to the headshaven ones), when suddenly I slipped, caught hold of the column and slid down it straight onto the two of them and their chessboard, scattering the pieces all over the floor.

Naturally, you apologized profusely and scrabbled busily about on the stone tiles looking for those tiny bits of wood, as it seemed at first.

The chessmen were homemade. The chessboard, an ordinary plywood box that had been diligently, if somewhat coarsely, put together, had darkened with age so that the black and white squares differed little one from the other. A variety of stains and lines had appeared on them as a result of the frequent application and no less frequent removal of varnish; pictures and whole landscapes appeared there, resembling mysterious maps and certainly containing a secret record of good moves. Of course, the chessmen proved to be of the most varied kinds; they belonged to different sets and had been in various hands. There were strange beasts—half knights and half rooks whose role in the game you could not fathom, you also saw traditional horses' heads, but they could hardly have belonged to the chess cavalry, for they had no base and could not stand upright but terminated below in four straight horns like those used by embroiderers to make flowers out of thread. One of the bishops was an ordinary tin soldier in a 1940s Red Army uniform, the other a Chinese monk carrying seven spheres, one fitted inside the next; beside the bishop there was, instead of the rook, a ceramic checkers piece, and opposite it a die that was carved in black ivory and for some reason had six

dots on each face. Alongside a cheap poker counter I saw an exotic and undoubtedly valuable item that was certainly too big for the chessboard squares. From the front it was a Buddhist temple, and on the reverse was a representation of the Christmas crib with the Holy Family. Under someone's bag I found a pencil sharpener in the form of a green plastic frog. It, too, served as a chessman. I had collected quite a lot of this stuff—much more than was needed for the game—but still I had not found a single king or queen. The pawns were the worst. They were all of different sizes (often they were just bishops with their heads screwed off), and they had rolled into the most unexpected places. Children, faster and more agile than I, had already begun playing with some of them. Others I had simply overlooked at first, for in the absence of real pawns buttons and coins had been used, and, worst of all, plasticine balls coated with varnish. Many of these I had simply squashed with my knees. Now, after detaching them from my trousers, I rolled them into spheres again and gave them back to their owners, apologizing once more. The damage could not be undone, for the balls were not as beautiful and shiny the second time around. All sorts of rubbish adhered to them, and they stuck to my hands. So I was very pleased whenever I found these strange pod-like pawns undamaged. But soon it became clear that after my fall there had appeared on the floor, who knows from where, a large number of grape berries, plump and of an excellent variety, not unlike black Muscat, and in my ignorance I had been gathering these instead of the ill-fated plasticine balls. That made me
more and more
unpopular with my swarthy hosts.

The Great Flood

That One did not like talking about the great flood and did so laconically. Because he was obliged to do so often, much more often than he would have liked, he had worked out a certain narrative scheme from which he never deviated.

He began, as a rule, by describing the landscape around Briukhovychi,[36] very similar to the one that exists in reality, but a little different, as if touched up for an advertising photograph, with more contrast and brighter colors. Photos of that kind are always taken from a particular angle chosen with professional dishonesty, and when, driven by unconscious and sublimated desires, you end up in those parts for real, echt, live, you can never see them as the photographer has represented them. You walk about disappointed and a bit ashamed at having fallen, once again, for the multicolored and well-preserved advertising bait, and to cut your losses you try to find a place, a hillock or tree, from which reality would have the appearance you need. But as a rule you can't manage this trick—the devil knows how the photographer does. Perhaps he uses special lenses or takes the photographs from a helicopter hovering a meter above the ground. Then there is the effect of the limited field of vision. After all, you cannot see beyond the edge of a postcard, where there is probably a garbage dump or a tedious outdoor cafe or a crowd of bored wet tourists who have come running at the sound of the helicopter and now try desperately to get into the picture as they dry themselves in the streams of hot air propelled by the rotor blades.

That is how it was in That One's stories. The hillocks suddenly became taller, the slopes steeper, the valleys more picturesque. From the road leading to the bridge (next to which, flanked by a forest, stood my late grandfather's house) you could see all three lakes, clearer and bluer than in life, as well as the cemetery, grandfather's grave, the church, obscured by pine trees, and, quite implausibly, the railway line.

In That One's story there was one other not quite intelligible detail—a hint at underground tunnels of some kind. They might have been gigantic water pipes, or the lines of an unfinished subway going all the way to Lviv (where at a certain time the water table began to fall and buildings to settle and crack). Some said that through them you could get to the Poltva, and therefore into the city's sewers, and therefore into anyone's apartment. But these rumors remained no more than rumors, and That One did not overburden his narrative with them.

The great flood caught him on a forested slope that descends straight to the house next door. From a distance you could even look into our windows, and That One swore that he had seen Grandfather alive there. Down below (up the street, that is) our neighbor was carrying stuff out of her house and bringing in the cows.

I tried feverishly to recollect the true arrangement of the neighbors' yard (in order to divide truth from darkness)—the arrangement of the chicken coops, stables and sties, the paths to the ever migrating outhouse, to the gates, to the ancient German pump that, after long and exhausting exertions on your part, would maliciously spit out a portion of brackish, muddy and yet indescribably delicious water. But memory, though it rewarded me generously with vivid and exact details, lied godlessly about proportions and dimensions. I could imagine the yard only very approximately, and every time it seemed different. I saw it now from the low perspective of a cat or chicken, now as if I were growing steeply upward. I imagined it tiled with pre-Bolshevik brick, strong as steel. I imagined the tall meshwork of the wire fence that supported but now barely restrained the heavy flesh of the sandy slope that overhung the yard (endeavoring, ever more indecently, to rupture that frail corset) and, last of all, the path, steep and impossible to climb without slipping on the pine needles at least once and tearing the skin from the palms of your hands, whose grasping reflex was always somewhat delayed. (Yours or your hands'?)

There is no escaping the pine gum that makes your fingertips unhappily sticky. (Yes?)

None shall escape socks filled with sand that grinds your feet to dust and grit. (On wormwood graves.)

(Pause)

Memory can never recreate everything, but the words arranged above suffice to let us envisage That One at the very top of the slope where he was caught by the great flood, as announced.

There he is, clinging to the trunk of a tree and observing with horror as a resistless and hitherto unknown river bursts from the tangle of the forest and, sweeping away everything in its path, cascades downhill toward the houses, the road, the people, the lakes, the rivers and streams, the graves and crosses.

It is much more difficult to imagine the water itself. This turbulent seething torrent, carrying sand and trees and stones and cattle and birds and bushes and rubbish and prayers and blasphemies, effortlessly gouges a channel through soil as loose as peeled barley, altering the landscape in an instant, shaping cliffs and precipices at its somnambulous and shifting banks.

It is difficult also because in this part of the story That One's vocabulary would begin to bristle with wordy and stilted clichés and platitudes that might have been borrowed from cheap adventure novels. The rampage of natural forces depicted with the aid of such uncertain and devalued devices came across as somewhat unpersuasive and caricatured, but the fear experienced by That One, which smoldered in his eyes even now, spoke for itself and, better than words, conveyed the spasm of despairing stupefaction with which That One had embraced the pine tree, an unreliable and accidental friend in need.

(Pause)

The edge of the riverbank came remorselessly closer, the ground crumbled away down the cliff, the river swirled and roared below, and some ten meters remained to the end of That One's days. But suddenly, it was hard to say from where (at this point That One's lexicon returned to normal), there appeared among the trees on the slope a boy aged ten or twelve, cradling a wolf cub in his arms. The boy was completely unperturbed, the apocalyptic scene appeared not to trouble him at all, he looked the trembling That One up and down with a certain skepticism or, indeed, disdain, walked around on the edge of the slope as if choosing a convenient place, and then, with a hearty whoop and a whistle, leapt up and, holding the cub in his arms, slid deftly down the wet clay and the pine needles as children slide down a snow-covered hill in winter.

(Here I should note that my point of view, which earlier had almost entirely coincided with That One's, suddenly changed. It was as if I had slid down with the boy and the two of us were now looking up at That One from below. Furthermore, with a logic characteristic only of dreams, the riverbank, the slope, the points of the compass—indeed, the whole panorama—had turned ninety degrees, but the river, oddly enough, had not bothered to change its direction, in keeping, no doubt, with the same weird logic.)

The boy came agilely to a halt at the very edge of the water, put down the wolf cub, which immediately busied itself exploring the place, and began idly throwing pine cones, sticks, stones, and other debris into the river. He soon tired of this undemanding task and started helping the torrent demolish the bank. He raked at the soil with his hands (it was wet and sandy) and laughed with pleasure as each successive layer slid down onto him and his four-legged friend. The puppy, too, seemed to enjoy this sport. It would leap about, growl fiercely at the various streams and showers of sand, then get out from under the landslip, shake itself, and be ready for more games.

But That One felt no joy. Timidly looking over his shoulder, he could see the edge of the cliff creeping toward him before his very eyes (the aberrant perspective that I have mentioned, as well as a certain confusion in proportions, caused the height that for the boy was trivial and easily scaled to expand for That One into an insurmountable and fatal obstacle). Another minute, perhaps, and he would fall into the abyss together with his tree and, should death fail to come during the fall, it would certainly lurk for him below, among the black and unclean waves.

He understood then that he wanted to save himself.

That One's thoughts on the ways of salvation, as reported by himself, repeatedly alluded, chorus-like, to a mysterious subterranean realm of mystic water pipes and a more than hypothetical subway system. "If," he thought, "I could swim underwater to the central reservoir (which, though imaginary, rapidly moved closer in keeping with the laws of this phantom and capricious realm and now took its place almost directly under Granddad's house), then I could follow the tunnels—they never get more than three-quarters full (the devilishly clever ventilation system was calculated to ensure that air collecting in the tunnel would exert a residual pressure, preventing the water from rising above a certain level)—to Lviv and come to the surface in one of the reservoirs on High Castle Hill, the Ararat of these lands."

But to carry out such a plan he had to stay alive for at least a few seconds in the slurry of water, trees, rocks, etc. (see above), and this seemed impossible. So That One decided to pursue the boy instead.

This required suitable preparations.

Without letting go of the tree, he tried to dislodge a wedge of earth with his foot. This proved surprisingly easy, perhaps because his attempt coincided with an exertion by the boy, who was still playing below. This time the mass of soil was so great that it covered the child almost up to his chest, and the puppy disappeared under the landslide altogether. The poor kid began feverishly digging, trying to get himself out and save the wolf cub, but That One would not let him. He pushed again with his foot, and another mass of earth rolled downward, and now only the boy's head remained above the surface. The little fellow screamed and wriggled his whole body (as far as one could see), trying to squirm his way up. There was little time left. Sensing that the tree was losing its stability and would soon collapse (its wide root system was already exposed), and still clinging to the trunk, That One jumped up and brought both feet down on the ground with all his might. A whole crag, no doubt several tons in weight, separated from the cliff and slid down, disintegrating as it went. It left a gentle and relatively smooth slope, with only a few broken branches sticking out here and there. Its mass pushed to one side the course of the river, which, as if sensing the power and might of dry land, began to sigh, retreat and go calm. Nothing that could be seen reminded one of the boy and the wolf cub, although at that moment both were probably just beginning to choke, less for lack of air than from claustrophobic horror and the dawning certainty of their merciless and slow end.

Nothing remained for That One to do but push himself away from the doomed and already tottering pine tree, leap aside with unexpected agility and complete his descent to safety, walking at first, then crawling on all fours, sinking elbows and knees into the loose earth.

On Morons

"Listen, he was a moron, right? Him and his pup. A moron pure and simple. People like him always grow up to be morons. I'm not a bit sorry for him. You think he'd change if he grew up? Fat chance. Morons! I know them by heart. I see them a mile off. I've seen so many, it makes me want to puke my soul up. Hell, buddy, I really hate those bastards.

A moron is never better entertained than when he sees someone trip and fall or a crow crap on someone's head or someone sit on a freshly painted bench or step into a puddle. Morons come in different varieties, but they will always be morons. The moron diligently belches after lunch, knowing you can't stand it, and laughs out loud if he sees you grimace in disgust. In his poetic reveries he cleans his fingernails with a comb, his ear with a matchstick and his teeth with a pair of scissors, the deliberately cultivated long yellow fingernail of his little finger, a paper clip or a safety pin. In puberty, without cease or respite, he squeezes zits in front of the mirror, and in the mating season he continuously exercises himself on his female, preferring to do so in frequented places, on the beach, for example. If a number of morons get together, they drink beer out of three-liter cans till they're blue in the face, then hold championships in the loud expulsion of body gases or writing in piss. Calligraphic skills notwithstanding, the moron's aim always misses the toilet and the urinal, not to mention the bedpan. But he loves to relieve himself in the sink. Those rare varieties of moron whom nature has endowed with sure aim never flush when they finish; they conclude the act of urination by throwing a cigarette butt into the yellow puddle.

In refectories or cafeterias the moron is incapable of traversing the distance to the cash register without drinking up his apple juice or starting to stuff himself with a sweet doughnut, waiting neither for the bill nor for dessert. And even if the apple juice manages somehow to survive to the end of the meal, the moron will only swallow it after first rinsing his mouth with it. I've seen morons who rinsed their gobs with buttermilk, black coffee, even champagne. This last, as a rule, ended in catastrophe.

The moron has an irrepressible affection for chewing gum. He finds it enormously hard to spit out and even harder to throw away. He prides himself on his ability to blow it into bubbles (those who can't do this console themselves by pulling it from between their teeth like long, calibrated strings of snot). When eating, kissing or engaging in official discussions the moron takes out his chewing gum and puts it in a visible place, so that all might admire the cast of his perfect jaw. In such situations the most refined roll the gum into a compact white ball and then attach it behind the ear. Morons stick used bits of gum, sucked dry until only their sticky essence remains, to chairs and walls, under tables and windows, in a word—everywhere.

The moron never uses a serviette prior to taking a drink. That is why glasses bearing the marks of his saliva and grease grace every festive table. Female morons—bimbos—generously smear the crockery with ineradicable traces of their water-, kerosene- and acetone-insoluble lipstick.

Bimbos are an altogether pathetic sight when eating. Evidently because of some as yet unresearched syndrome preventing coordinated movement, they constantly knock their teeth, damaged as they are to start with, with (with-with: remember that!) forks, spoons, and cups. Breakfasting with them is an acoustic fairy-drama, and dinner becomes a real dental bacchanal.

The bimbo is direct. More to the point, she is responsive to natural urges. When she comes to visit you in the evening, she has no thought of proceeding to copulation—not at all! She would never descend to such vulgar and pragmatic considerations. But at some point, surprising even herself, she suddenly falls on her back and spreads her legs wide, and you have the opportunity of enjoying all the aromas of her body, washed only the day before yesterday.

After a night with a bimbo you become the owner of terrifying monstrosities: mountains of lipstick-stained cigarette butts, an unexpectedly hirsute and curly-haired bar of soap (for in the end, to your misfortune, you make her take a bath), and suspicious novelties in your garbage can.

Signs of these importunate creatures' vital activities poison every part of your life:

they cut sausage with a knife just dipped in marmalade;

they pee without first closing the toilet door, evidently believing this really turns you on;

after a visit to the dentist they insist that you inspect the brand-new filling in the depths of their gaping maw and dismiss your cautious attempts to refuse, perceptively, as mere huffing and *puffing;*

their piquant habit of conversing at table allows you to follow in detail all the phases of the conversion of a schnitzel into *stuffing;*

their laughter is open, sincere and carefree, and as they laugh they display the contents of their nostrils and the blinding sheen of their gold crowns, irreversibly transforming your flirtation into a case of *bluffing;*

they can get excited about every little bird and every little cloud, they look for beauty in small things and worship various idols;

a piece of lettuce or spring onion invariably gets stuck between their teeth (what a stubborn motif!), rounding out a picture incomparable in color and texture: ebony and ivory, the virtuosity of crimson brushstrokes with the final accent of an emerald spot;

their used hygienic products can be encountered in the most impossible locations, including the peaks of high mountains (at least, every one of your seaside holidays has been poisoned by clumps of brownish cotton wool that stick out of all the cracks in the walls of those miserable changing huts where the children of morons cater to their various physiological needs);

like children, bimbos very elegantly chew sunflower seeds (for this their mouths open with a lasciviousness uncharacteristic of oral protuberances);

they drink beer with the enthusiasm of Gargantua, Pantagruel, Thomas Mann and his brother Heinrich all rolled into one;

with the delight of true philologists they hearken to bellows and curses;

their spit is as thick as a soldier's;

and they love reading, writing and singing;

and they know quotations;

and they know how to make love,

and this is truly and indubitably so, for loyalty and dedication, dedication and loyalty and infinite submissiveness imbue their love for their morons of the male sex.

Moron, moron, moron...

What else is there to say?

The moron is a man of principles in which he devoutly believes and to which he devoutly believes that he adheres. One cretin whose neighbor I was forced to be for several years and who transformed those years into a hell of cordial relations persuaded me in the space of a few minutes as he was saying his farewells that all his actions were governed by the laws of universal justice and harmony. And I understood how wrong and shortsighted I had been to regard him as a petty criminal and a vengeful villain.

The moron is always in favor of something-a-bit-original. He energetically pursues exotic, critical, extraordinary and marginal manifestations of being.

The moron is a great enthusiast of trips to the country. With barbecues, girls, and music.

The moron is generally moody and sometimes sentimental. He loves recalling his childhood and youth. Like a real snob, he makes cocktails according to recipes that he has read about in Papa Hemingway. And he drinks coffee at intervals suggested by the post-Eisensteinian montage characteristic of French films.

The moron is a born tourist. Every tour bus is bursting with morons.

Morons love talismans, badges and souvenirs of any kind, from postcards and pendants to ambassadorial credentials and family crests. A moron without a bracelet or a ring, an earring or a neckband, or perhaps a tattoo, or perhaps a pin in his lapel, or perhaps an anagram on his underwear is not a moron, or not quite a moron. I for one would submit that his claim to being a moron is inauthentic and dubious.

The moron is always an individualist. He stands out from the crowd. He has his own style, wears his hair and dresses in a manner uniquely his own, and carefully selects his shoes and accessories. That, probably, is why the crowd consists of morons.

The moron is keen on knowledge, indeed, on omniscience. He yearns for Wisdom, Verity and Truth (all this, as they say in Polish, in capital letters, of course). With his tiny arms he wants to embrace the whole world—with his foul-smelling, all-embracing love.

The moron is never satisfied with having just the one ancestral faith and craves always to comprehend all existing and imaginary religions. The moron is a researcher and an ecumenist. He is consumed by curiosity and sensory deprivation.

It was morons who instigated the first expeditions to the East (and the West), it was they who invented the words "siddharta," "catharsis," and "nirvana." It was they who introduced tomatoes, gunpowder and opium and compiled the first dictionary of mythology.

They fought for declarations of independence and of rights. They advocate equality and democracy. Everywhere they go they preach the word of God.

Morons created science and the so-called "objective approach," according to which black and white, top and bottom, sacred and profane, wine and shit, and it and it are all merely objects of classification and of equal value.

Morons are characterized by profound metaphoric and esoteric vision. They and only they can descry in earth and water, cave and cellar, chamber and tunnel, window and wreath, galoshes and socks symbols of the uterus, the womb, the vagina or, to put it bluntly, the c(...). It is they who perceive in the tree and the finger, the train and the violin bow, the arrow and the unicorn, the trombone, the pipe, the sausage, the cucumber and even the ballpoint pen the one great and invincible p(...).

Morons invented art and variously promote its cult. They claim to be no more than mediators of the harmony of the celestial spheres. Artists, they say, are the noblest and the most vulnerable part of humanity. When they carry on about their "raw nerves" and their *Weltschmerz* they can whip their public into such a frenzy that it nearly shits itself. The public loves to go into a frenzy like that. Artists have acquired special over-award rights to get smashed, laid, stoned, and high as a kite; to make love to other men's wives and their own mothers-in-law, to the legally underage, to senior citizens, to cloven-hoofed ungulates, laying fowls, marsupials, and cross-winged birds; they even have the right not to make love at all. They can't wring a chicken's neck but have no problem slashing their wrists on stage. There you have it—the liminal anguish of the inexpressibly self-sacrificial existence of the hypersensitive artistic heart!

But I'm getting carried away.

I think the moron is also scrupulous and ceremonious (or unscrupulously unceremonious) and, like every human being, sinful and weak.

And finally:

The moron, as a rule, is a good friend. That's why morons stick together. The moron cannot be by himself. Gregariousness overshadows all his other desires and instincts, even the instinct of self-propagation. Herds of indigenous morons are unusually stable. They have their own taboos and occupy more or less well defined territories. And therefore the eradication of morons would not be such a difficult problem. In fact, it's an eschatological problem, since practically everyone is a moron."

Siana

This lecture on morons was actually delivered by That One on a completely different occasion in a great university auditorium with no windows (but with two doors), where the desks ascending from the squat lectern bore a simplified resemblance to an amphitheater.

Truth to tell, it was not exactly this lecture, and the words were not exactly those that we have just savored. That was, rather, an angry, determined and turbulent speech against democracy, delivered by That One for the benefit of Siana, daughter of that breed of educated and sincere Ukrainians who were so charming and rare a while ago, and have now already become a bit tedious and ordinary—the kind that have a taste for folkloric vests, *trembitas* and Easter eggs, who decorate their quarters with Hutsul kilims and the Taras-Ivan-Lesia triad (in that order)[37] instead of paintings, and who customarily regard as their capital neither Kyiv nor Halych nor least of all Krylos, but Kolomyia[38] with its market and fair.

Siana, like most children of such true martyrs and true patriots, had run off to America some time ago and now materialized before That One only because she had come to see her daughter, whom solicitously she had left behind to absorb the aromas of the ancestral lands. Naturally, she had changed completely. Very little remained of that little girl a year older than you (she had joined your class late after some cardiac illness) who secretly brought you her sexually mature brother's Polish magazines with pictures of undressed ladies in them, as well as cassette recordings of Abba, Boney M and Smokey, and who asked you one day on the way home from school what words you knew that began with "p." After skeptically listening to the whole of your impoverished and chaste glossary, she mystically and solemnly enunciated a word, widely known for its laconic brevity, for the attempted publication of which, many years later, the ideological allies of Siana's parents would long pillory you on the pages of the sycophantic press. Now, having filled herself to bursting with American habits and liberties (without, however, parting with her folkloric vest), she already regarded the local way of life with a certain forgetful incomprehension, stared with disdain at the peeling walls of the university building (unlike their American counterparts, however, they were solid and soundproof) and marveled at the audience's imperturbable reserve, which she herself believed and proclaimed to be "the outcome of sexual complexes."

Oddly enough, the audience in fact consisted of your aging contemporaries, whom you—both of you—had run into all the time in the corridors and sports halls, on the meadows and pathways of your gleaming but fractured childhood.

At some point Siana said in a tired voice that she wouldn't mind drinking some grass. You did not mishear, you remember quite well that she said "drinking," not "smoking," though it was clear what she meant, and in response to your somewhat panicked surprise she informed you condescendingly that over there it was quite acceptable ("Don't we all smoke hashish in Montreal," she rhymed, breaking into a smile that might have accompanied the invitation "cheese"), at which point you, that's to say That One, that's to say you-that's-That One exploded in spit and outrage and for five or six minutes harangued this woman, liberated from complexes but exhausted by abstinence, demonstrating that nothing was more mendacious and revolting "than this much-lauded democracy of yours," that only egomaniacal idiots could believe in the wisdom of the working majority, that liberalism was nothing more than a variation on the heretical pride of a dullwitted orderly, that Siana's ratshit America was the hotbed of the world's evil and debauchery (actually, before you could say this last bit, you were cut short by a mutual acquaintance who came in late, boasting of a whole basket of mushrooms that she had collected nearby, in the university park, and the fervor with which you had been persuading Siana of the impossibility of popular sovereignty you now hurled into assuring the unfortunate mushroom picker that under no circumstances at all should one pick mushrooms within the city limits, nor medicinal herbs either, for the ground water here was poisoned by all possible chemicals and filth, and the ground was surely smothered with the most noxious possible combinations of toxic superheavy metals). But even this ecological interlude was interrupted. This time by the completely absurd appearance of your first schoolteacher, a malicious harridan whom, it seemed, years and the aging process had generously passed by, and who appeared looking like her former cutthroat self, but for some reason with a violin in her hand. (The original of that tormentress of yours would not even have known how to hold the instrument.) Quite at ease, she tapped the music stand with her bow and, having no expectation of calming these grown-up retards by other means, belted out a simple and jolly Jewish melody that you could not identify but recognized with a sleepwalker's casual disdain as a motif from *Fiddler on the Roof.*

That would seem to be everything worth mentioning in connection with the lecture on morons, which came about as an explanation and justification of the willful murder of a boy and his wolf cub, which itself could have happened, indubitably, only in consequence of the coming of the deep and eternal flood.

Paradise

Yet water, or more precisely the motif of water, does not end with the Great Flood of Briukhovychi, for you remember well your fabulous journeys along the magical banks of the old Dnipro—the glorious Dnipro, swollen somewhat by rumor, whose center can be reached only by the most audacious and hardiest of avians[39] (and on both sides of which, let me add, there are neither cities nor settlements, especially none such as the aforementioned and godforsaken Kyiv)[40]—looking for that sublime, song-celebrated sanatorium, that white-columned Arcadia, that Livadia,[41] that meadow where in the shimmering shade of junipers and cypresses reposed maidens translucent and pure, perfect in heart and body, their skin exquisite with the down that, in the words of the entomological Grand Master, "swaddles the fruit of trees of the almond group."[42]

These quests for paradise in the fairy-tale garden along the Dnipro slipped from your memory for a time, until one afternoon there appeared in a daydream, like a reproach, a vision from those dreams of long ago, and then (apparently, even in your absence the stubborn quest had not ceased for a moment) the action shifted to the health farm, which, it turned out, had been found after all and was an Eden you had already conquered and now inhabited.

True, on closer inspection the maidens of your dreams proved to be none other than the tiresome girls from your old class, and the frolics and pleasures of paradise nothing but some sort of canoe race for which everyone dutifully trained. As usual, you ended up with a dreadful, rickety and unsafe tub—a ruin that might have been gouged out of a rotten log by some denizen of Cro-Magnon or other.[43] It also leaked. A hole drilled by some unknown miscreant gaped right in the middle of the wretched craft, which probably for that reason came equipped with a rusty tin for bailing water. So while others assiduously practiced their oar work, you practiced staying afloat and bailing the water out faster than it came in, spurred on by your zit-faced, fat-legged classmates. (For safety's sake you stayed close to the bank, often holding on to the unplaned planks of the pier.)

The time of the race was fast approaching.

Yet all this was of no import, for already true happiness, the pure light of heavenly joy filled you to the brim, it overflowed you, doomed as you were to defeat and perhaps to death, it overflowed all possible brims and splashed onto the calm, flat surface of the river, onto the already wet boat, the pier, the unprepossessing girls, the green riverbanks, the health farm and the whole wide world, and so grateful were you for this gift of infinite generosity, this quiet glow of beatitude, that in your gratitude you woke up in tears (so that was the objective correlative of the joyful damp!) and began at once to recite, one after another, your passionate and earnest

prayers

which even now you wish you were able to recite as you wish that the night would pass more quickly, this dark and stupid and solitary night; that it would go, pass by, fly away, and with it would disappear your pain and, God willing, you yourself would end, and only dreams would have no pause or end at all—nowhere, not ever, not for any cause.

"Our Father, Which art in Heaven, hallowed be Thy Name, Thy Kingdom come, Thy will be done on earth as it is in Heaven. Give us this day our daily bread, and forgive us our trespasses as we forgive them that trespass against us. And lead us not into temptation, but deliver us from evil. For Thine is the Kingdom, the power and the glory, now and forever. Amen.
Lord Jesus Christ, have mercy on me
Lord Jesus Christ, have mercy on me
Lord Jesus Christ, have mercy on me
Lord Jesus Christ,
have mercy on me
Lord
Jesus Christ,
have mercy on me
Lord
Jesus
Christ, have mer
cy on
m e
Lo
rd Je sus
Chri
s t, h a
ve me
r
c
y
o n m e

Chapter Two

DAY

Coming Down

Why down, exactly? Do you really believe those pagan tales about the soul flying high at night and returning to the body before morning? Coming down? You would be the first to argue that sleep is a fluid—melted amber or translucent rosin; that to sleep is to dive. Not to fly. And not even to dive but to submerge yourself gradually. And not even to submerge yourself but rather to be submerged by this warm languor. It will cover first your ears, then your eyes and nostrils, and then rise slowly until you find yourself at the bottom of the deepest ocean trench, where there is probably no life, or where in the silence of the watery darkness creatures waft past that are as relic-like as they are unreal—holothurians, ascidians, ophiuroids,[44] sea lilies—carried by underwater currents or their own imagination.

No, sleep is not a fluid. Was it not you who once wrote, "I shall burrow my way into sleep as into dust"? Sleep is a warm, dry substance consisting of finely ground minerals. Dust, in other words. The thick midday dust on the path you walked as a boy to get to the river, on either side of which (both path and river) poison ambrosia grew in abundance. To this day you remember how good your feet felt walking on that dust (it was probably like the clouds over which the heroes of Renaissance paintings so confidently stroll), and what a trial it was for your tender child's foot to cross a strip of oil-smeared asphalt or a graveled yard or a clearing overgrown with coarse southern grass. (Another unpleasant tactile experience was returning home to the concrete courtyard. That courtyard was always in the dense shade of the grapevine, and the cold of the concrete was, if not exactly otherworldly, certainly suggestive of another climate. Just as cold was the floor of the house where once, deciding to explore your grandfather's wardrobe, you found a beautiful crystal box. It was triangular and had a copper latch, quirkily curved legs and a velvet lining in which you could discern something pink. You almost died from a sudden access of revulsion when you opened it and unwittingly picked up an old worn-out set of false teeth.)

(This happened in the South, where your other grandfather lived—not the one from Briukhovychi.)

Though perhaps one should look for parallels not so much material as spatial. Perhaps dreams are chasms into which your consciousness periodically trips and falls. Then, in order to return, you have to clamber up, not down, grasping at uncertain bushes, resting your weight on uncertain stones, passing *scraps of mist* as you go.

And yet, coming down. Dawn. Day.

Awakenings

Awakenings, too, would require classification if they could retain their variety independent of the sleeper's age. But their variety becomes more uniform with the passing of the years, and he no longer entertained any hopes of waking, as once he had, in tears of terror, let alone joy. And even though the transition from the life of the night to mundane being took place in the most varied circumstances and situations, a certain regularity emerged ever more distinctly: the awakenings demanded recapitulation.

The day (that is, the night) he broke the fourteen-hour barrier he somehow ended up in a not very wholesome bar—let's be frank, it was a vile and smelly snake pit, where he had the opportunity of singing "Hotel California" with the Eagles. And it went so well, and with such verve, and it was so great and so cool and so groovy that it would have been a sin not to play it again, whether for an encore or for their own pleasure. And so they played it again. And then, after the final solo, when the guitar fades out in a sweet arpeggio, the percussion of its own accord belted out that marvellous break—you know it?—Tum-barum-pum-bum-tum, and off we went for a third time, that wasn't bad either, and then a fourth and a fifth. The atmosphere in the crowded premises became red-hot, the audience—all those little drunks, vagrants and junkies—turned into a single family with one passion, one rhythm, one step, it felt as if there had never been any other music in the world, nor could there be, for the music of the spheres itself suddenly descended to this sinful earth and entered this poverty-stricken manger, and the only possible desire was that this should go on as long as possible.

And it did. It went on for a long time. He could not remember how many times he intoned that "Welcome to the Hotel California"—a hundred? a thousand? He was aware only that this was a dream, definitely a dream, most probably a morning dream (for even the dazed listeners had gradually crept away to their places of shelter, and the hungover cleaning woman had begun to give them disgruntled looks as she knocked over chairs and slopped water around the filthy floor, and still you played one and the same thing as if bewitched, while outside morning had long been rolling in), in addition he felt, odd though this was, that sleep time corresponded to real time—the time that was in force out there, on the other side, in actuality, in the so-called real world. And therefore over there, too, light was pouring in through the windowpane; there, too, a new day was beginning, and it was high time to wake up. But there is no possibility of breaking through, of surfacing from that unstable stiff brew of sleep, because the spiral of the plot, like the groove of a scratched record, is broken and has become a circle, and the ear repeatedly catches that "tum-barum-pum-bum-tum," by now painfully ingrained, while "Welcome to the Hot..." keeps on breaking loudly from your throat.

Who knows, perhaps he might not have woken up then, perhaps he might have remained suspended in that eternal concert, had it not been for the telephone. Murmuring something into the receiver, still in English phonetics, he glanced at the clock and noted with some displeasure that he had not broken the fourteen-hour barrier after all. "Damn," he thought—as if he had not yearned a moment ago to return to consciousness—"why didn't it ring ten minutes later? We'd have sung it through twice more, and the thing would have been done."

After that incident he developed the habit of covering his head with a pillow.

There were also
recurrals of curs
and recurrences of returns.

You returned quite often to places where you had been before—to the parkland on the banks of the Dnipro, for example, or the city of your childhood, or another city, the refuge of your youth—attesting the existence beyond memory of a complete landscape of your dreams. A landscape that, naturally, was mutable, capricious, dynamic and unstable, and yet had fairly coherent borders, coordinates, demographic indices, population centers and topography.

(And so it was that Wozzeck, who possessed the priceless gift of providential guidance in small things, noticed a year or two before inheriting a property on the outskirts of the city that the confused plots of his dreams brought him ever more frequently to a neglected building in the depths of an abandoned park. It had no architecture (except for a few details—a windowsill burned by cigarette butts, a bit of wall with a solitary nail driven into it, a piece of loose parquetry), and everything was of one ubiquitous color: the sour, cloudy hue of the old photographs in his father's album. The characters who inhabited this building and the stories that unfolded there or, rather, the traces of these stories all had the color of a quivering, misty, moldy emulsion.)

So the world existed. Whether it was the world of quantum physics or a world infernal or neurophysiological mattered little to you, yet you dreamed of maps of this world. They would help you keep your bearings on your travels, but there was no sense in trying to make these maps during the day, whereas those you sketched in secret at night were confiscated without fail by invisible customs officers as you crossed the frontier of dreams. The world of dreams really was a world of ceaseless, unambiguous and implacable metamorphoses: returning there, you always caught yourself feeling that your language, behavior, habits and even dress were already somehow anachronistic. Naturally, you always tried to adjust to that world as quickly as you could, but even so people looked at you now with resentment, now with astonishment, and you yourself were sometimes surprised to learn of changes that had happened in the law, or the rules of etiquette, or fashion. You were haunted by the sense that you had missed something important, something essential, that you would never be completely accepted if you continued flitting incessantly between the realms of day and of night. Nor did you feel out there, in the light up above (or, more precisely, down below), that you were in your own element, for while you wandered aimlessly through parks and cities, singing yourself hoarse with the Eagles or killing boys and their wolf cubs, the ones up there (more precisely, down here), whoever they were, were not asleep or sitting on their hands, either. That was why you were always nervous when you woke up and went out. Was your veteran's pass still valid? Were your clothes not too much of a provocation? Was today by any chance a public holiday or, rather, a day of national mourning, and here you were, you ignoramus, barging out into the street in white trousers and a checked shirt.

So there you are, tearing yourself between two homelands like Buridan's ass,[45] for whom the right not to choose was dearer even than food.

Awakenings Continued

A certain Sasha Abramian,[46] among others, suggested reprises of another kind. Sasha was in your year at the Institute (crazy language! how can you be "in" a year?). Everyone simply called him Abrasha, not so much because of his Semitic background as to punish him for excessive zeal in the Komsomol and, later, in the party. On the whole he was not a bad guy, even if he was a collaborator. One day he even brought to the dear old alma mater a whole stack of *Playboy* magazines, still banned at the time, and you perused them with much delight right next to the bust of some party luminary or other. But, who knows, maybe that was a special kind of provocation. (After the fall of the regime, Abrasha surfaced in Lviv as the leader of the Armenian National Front—wasn't that just typical for a KGB stool pigeon?) Anyway, десять років тому in one of your dreams the two of you met in that selfsame hall next to that selfsame bust and in exactly similar circumstances: Abrasha had a stack of glossy magazines in his arms. Except that this time the magazines were a bit different—more explicit, of course (society had, after all, become more liberal), rather more pedantic and, what is more, of a certain orientation. Why beat around the bush? The magazines were for queers. You didn't twig straight away to what was going on and what this shit was for. Whatever else you liked, you didn't like looking at gay men. Abrasha made a roundabout speech about Michelangelo and his

David, the beauty of the male body and the aesthetics of brotherly love, Tchaikovsky and Gide, Caravaggio, Mercury,[47] Wilde and Kost Hnatenko,[48] the New York artistic elite and human loneliness, the difficulty of communication and the need for tenderness until you spat with anger and headed for the exit, sending him to the devil. That was the point where everything went weird. The main building of the Polytechnic turned out to be an absolutely faithful reconstruction of that gigantic hotel, the Grand, where you once searched for the washroom and had the unpleasant adventure with the chessmen. And you got lost in exactly the same way among the balustrades and passageways. And although this time there were men's toilets all over the place, they gave you little joy, for in each lurked Abrasha with his sad and eloquent look. He stepped out from behind columns and corners, materialized in various niches, turned up among the students who poured out of the auditoriums from time to time, touched your shoulder as you bent over a drinking fountain, called out to you from balconies, caught up with you on staircases—in a word, was omnipresent and indestructible. (It had long been an axiom that the characters in your nightmares were a priori indestructible, yet you could rarely resist temptation and now rushed insanely to kill, kill, kill, kill the one who so easily and triumphantly had come back to life.) And so Abrasha was transformed into his own endless reprise. You yelled at him, hurled your foulest curses at him, spat on him, you ran ever faster, doors slammed, windows flashed past, you found yourself on other floors (only the color of the walls and the pattern of the floor tiles told you where you were), yet everywhere he was present, Abrasha with his message of brotherly love. You snatched the magazines from his hands and flung them down the stairs and punched him in the jaw, but your punch was somehow feeble, because, as usually happens in dreams, your hand would neither clench itself firmly into a fist nor maintain the right direction or force. It turned out to be not much of a blow. Still, it was the only way of getting rid of this tiresome pederast, so you gathered all your available willpower, all the strength you had, you strained so hard that some small part of your consciousness almost woke up with all that straining, came to consciousness of itself as a true "I" and began analyzing you, or rather your somnolent protagonist: "Gather yourself together and concentrate as much as you can. Your problem is not to beat Sasha-Abrasha, your problem is to conquer sleep." But sleep proved more powerful than the watchful analyst, and you ended up fighting Abrasha—with some success, too, because you began to feel your opponent's body going soft and your fist making quite serious indentations in his flesh. You kept on bashing him and bashing him with a brutality you had never shown before, until you suddenly realized that you were beating an inflatable doll from the sex shop, and that the doll was already half deflated. That, and not any strength on your part, was the reason for its softness. In the shock of it all you froze and stared like a sheep at that monster of a homunculus and its already semiamorphous synthetic body in the middle of which, the last bastion of artificial life, was an already drooping elastic plastic (elastic plastic!) phallus.

But even this was not enough for the dream's insane director. Yet another metamorphosis took place, and suddenly you felt that you were inside the body of the doll. You lay, battered, half your life had gone out with half your air, you were a victim of your own violence, you autopygmalion, you theseominotaur. You felt yourself dying. In this world the only thing that awaited you was death. And only such a death. And there was no way around this, nor would there ever be, because:

The reprises, the reprises, the damned reprises, the loops and circles and traps of reprises.

You barely managed to open your eyes and raise your eyelids, perhaps for the last time, you thought, and—can you believe it?—it was this that saved you. Your gaze broke through to reality, and through the mists of retreating sleep you recognized your own room, your bed, your own body and even that thing, the last bastion of authentic life that stood half-upright, gladly welcoming the return of the master.

But not all adventures ended happily with a morning erection.

The Liubansky Syndrome

A night spent at Karp Liubansky's home shed light, or rather darkness, on the limitless lodes of the virtual vitality of night.

You were to leave early in the morning, so it was no surprise that your sleep in the unfamiliar bed should be restless. You could not help listening all the time for the voices of Karp's wife and children in the anteroom; these would signify that it was already morning and that your host would soon rise and come to wake you. Strictly speaking, because there was no chance of oversleeping, you had no need to be alert, but such was your sensitive and nervous nature. In the words of the beloved *Großmeister*, "What a guy, writing all night, not a moment's rest, how very interesting and pallid!"[49] Except that you, that's to say That One, that's to say you-That One, did no writing, you just slept, even if your sleep was troubled.

The objects of his keen expectations—voices in the anteroom—solicitously presented themselves, counterfeited, of course, by the omnipotent spirit of darkness. All night long he dreamed of one and the same thing: of being asleep and hearing voices in his sleep and knowing that soon it would be time to get up, but a sweet early morning drowsiness stopped him from waking up completely, although he badly wanted to rise early so that his host, on looking into the room, would find him clothed and ready. The dream repeated itself with such tedium and regularity that sleep became pointless. Rather than persisting with this agony he decided that he would be better off waking up and reading a book or something. Whatever it took, he would open his eyes, reach for the switch and turn on the light. But the same sweet drowsiness of what pretended to be the early morning would not allow it. After a long struggle he finally came to, turned on the light and looked at his watch. Something was not quite right. The watch itself and the band were the same as usual, but there should have been a crack in the glass (he had broken it helping a friend move some furniture), whereas this glass seemed undamaged. Obvious carelessness on the part of the dream's props master. "Aha, caught them out," thought That One, having in mind the invisible demiurges.[50] "I'm not so easily tricked." And, realizing that he was still asleep, he determined to wake up once and for all. Now he quite easily opened his eyes, immediately found the switch, narrowed his eyes against the bright light and once again cast a glace at the watch. This time everything was fine. Four a.m. Well then, better a book than these silly games. He looked around, expecting to see bookshelves, but instead saw that he was in a completely unfamiliar place—a spacious white hall with a wall of windows and a draft gently moving the curtains. "Damn you," he cursed furiously, "you've tricked me after all. But this is the last time." In his anger he sat up bolt upright in his bed and rubbed his face vigorously with his hands. Then he looked out the window—and froze. Everything was normal. It was Liubansky's apartment all right, the bookshelves were in place, the watch was fine, there was no reason even to check, but over there, beyond the glass of the balcony door, loomed a huge concrete idol. It was, without exaggeration, gigantic (Karp lived on the ninth floor). It stood impassively in the middle of a building lot, floodlit, encrusted in scaffolding, surrounded by the filigree outlines of construction cranes, and the shadows played so quirkily on its fearsome head that it seemed to stare straight into your eyes. "Damn! Why didn't I notice it yesterday in the daytime?" wondered That One, somewhat shaken. "I walked right past the place." On looking more closely he saw that it was the head of a helmeted warrior atop an immensely tall pedestal. Well, you could more or less understand that—the anniversary of the country's liberation was coming up, so it would be quite natural to put up a monument of some kind. But how, how could he fail to notice something like that? They couldn't have put it up overnight. That One had no doubt at all that what was happening was real. He did not even pinch himself in the arm—this gesture, typical of the dupe of fiction, would have been laughable now. Instead he got up, walked back across the room to the door and looked. Everything was in its place. The anteroom, the coat stand, the corridor. No reason to wake his hosts. That One went to the kitchen for a drink of water. He all but smashed the cup, catching it just short of the floor so awkwardly that it dropped again, but he had interrupted the fall, and the cup was saved. He listened anxiously. All quiet. Going back, he looked at himself in the mirror. Nothing unusual. He returned.

The idol had not moved.

"Let's think logically," said That One to himself, dividing himself, as was his wont, into simpleton and analyst. "If I'm still dreaming—and there's no point in dismissing that possibility—there's got to be a slipup somewhere. If it's a mystification, it can't be flawless. They don't have the time for that, and they're not exactly perfectionists. If I'm not dreaming, on the other hand,"—he had paused at a bookshelf and was leafing through some books, familiar books from Karp Liubansky's library, ones he had often seen, and there was not even a hint of anything wrong—"if I'm not dreaming, I've gone mad."

After much thought he decided that the best solution, since the idol refused to disappear, would be to go back to sleep and then take things as they came. God's will be done.

Tossing and turning in bed, he kept searching for the slipup. He wondered whether it might lie in the ease with which he had believed the phantom to be real, but this brought him no solace, and he could not get to sleep but was overcome instead by a heavy and anxious drowsiness, and he had begun gradually to slide into the muddy stream of that drowsiness when the life-saving solution came of its own accord. He remembered: there was a glassed-in loggia on Karp Liubansky's balcony, whereas the idol gazed straight through the pane of the balcony door. They had forgotten the loggia! They had, but he had not. Lord, how simple! In his joyful excitement the remnants of his drowsiness flew from him together with his blanket, he leapt up onto his bed and saw that he was right: a glassed-in loggia and no idols! A glassed-in loggia and no idols! His joy knew no bounds. He had prevailed! It was done!

The night was beginning to turn gray. The clock showed half past seven. Soon it would be time to get up. And there would be no need to listen for voices.

But there really were voices in the next room. Some of them That One could even identify.[51] To start with, of course, there was Karp Liubansky's voice with its patriarchal intonations. And that high-pitched one with the giggly laugh was probably Irpinets. And that little nasal bass was Gustav (which of them?). And that arrogant baritone was undoubtedly Borakne. And the muttering was surely Kamidian's. And the hysterical jabber of tongue-twisters surely belonged to Zabuzhko, the blithe patter to Lysheha, and the rolling laughter to combatant Dovhy... That One recognized almost all of them. The only thing that made him uneasy was why that whole bunch should be going on the trip with him. Now, quite close to the door, Karp intoned,

"And where's Hrytsenko?" It appeared that they had found Hrytsenko, for next came Liubansky's excessively loud and theatrical announcement, obviously intended as a warning, "And what about dear old That One? Could he still be asleep?" And at that moment the door sprang open, and the whole garrulous crowd flooded into the room—Karp, Karp's children and wife, and Irpinets and Borakne and Kamidian, and Irpinets's Oksana, Protsiuk, Malkovych, Andrusiak, Herasymiuk, Zabuzhko, Izdryk, Bryhynets, Hrytsenko and Rymaruk and Luhosad and just plain Sad, Lysheha, the Tsyperdiuks (Ivan and Dima), Fishbein, Lybon, Avzhezh and Pozaiak. They surrounded the bed, laughing loudly and pointing their fingers at That One. Their laughter seemed not at all benign. That One lay naked, for his blankets had dropped to the floor. He lay on his belly, unable even to raise his head, and the crowd around him laughed uproariously, as if they had lost their senses. "How did they get to stand all around the bed?" he thought feebly. "It was up against the wall. And what's wrong with my head? I've got to raise my head. At any cost. And look them in the eye. Then they'll disappear into fuck-all. They're not real. Come on, scum, raise your head! Now!"

Tearing his head with an immense effort from the pillow, still unseeing and wreathed in sleep, That One cast his gaze forward. Then he turned over on his back and lay for a time with his eyes closed, getting his breath back. It was morning. The damned night was probably over. He could hear Karp's wife in the anteroom getting the children ready for school. That One looked at his watch, noting almost intuitively now that the glass was cracked and therefore authentic. He could stay in bed for another ten minutes. What a crazy night. Idols, poets—the weird things you dream up!

A door slammed, and Karp Liubansky's booming voice could be heard, then the splash of water and the clatter of crockery, and talk in the anteroom. That One waited for the children to leave so that he, too, could wash and get his things ready. He had to tell Karp about these nocturnal adventures. Sheer literature. Or psychoanalysis. The children were not leaving. Karp's voice again. "Where's the big suitcase, do you know?" Talking to his wife. Probably time to get dressed. Tired as a dog. Never mind, he would catch some sleep on the train. "JUST A MINUTE, WHERE'S

MY CLOWN? WHERE THE HELL IS MY RED CLOWN?" Karp suddenly yelled. "I CAN'T GO WITHOUT A GIFT!" That One went cold with fright. Freezing, slimy dread filled his brain. The stuffed red clown was right here under the bed. His, That One's, bed. And if one thing was certain, it was that the clown had a close family relationship to the stone idol from the last nightmare but one.

After that, That One lost all count of his fictitious awakenings. The dreams fitted one into the next like matryoshka dolls or magic Chinese spheres. There was no end to them. And each time the imitation of reality was more complete, more perfect, and there was no hope of an end to this diabolical carousel.

And when the genuinely real Karp Liubansky woke you up by reciting poems—an old ritual between friends (was it Notnabokov on this occasion?)—you merely waved your arms at him feebly, muttered "Away, spook!" and turned over onto your other side.

After all, who knows? Maybe you were right, and that treacherous dream continues to this day.

Acoustics

Sound penetrates into consciousness as one of the first (messengers of the new day).

The earliest buses come around five. Each one—and at that time of day they are fairly rare—causes a slight ringing in the dining-room cabinet. It does not wake you but makes you incorporate into your current dream some reflections on a unique tectonic phenomenon: the palpable link between the tarmac of the highway that passes three hundred meters from your building (through layers of road metal and sand, through earth befouled by pipes, telephone cables and sewers, through suspect foundations and no less dubious walls, through the panels that serve you as a floor and your neighbors below as a ceiling, through the floorboards and the red timber of the cabinet) and the resonant crystal of wineglasses and a carafe that contains exactly three-quarters of a liter of any beverage, preferably alcoholic.

Those same buses moving at speed generate a distant melodic hum that is easily confused with the buzz of a nearby mosquito, especially if you have covered your head with a pillow, and that is the only way that you can get to sleep these days, the only way. This does not wake you either, but it makes you incorporate into your current dream (like dialogue dubbed into an animated film) reflections on the topic of sound in general. (Reflections in dreams: what arrogance!)

Wasps had made a nest below his bedroom window. They had apparently infested cracks in the wall, gaps between bricks and the small space for which the sheet-metal windowsill served as a roof. Falling asleep, he could hear a buzzing and rustling that seemed to come from inside the room, so close were the wasps to the inner surface of the wall. The secret nocturnal life of these insects fascinated him. His imagination painted dim and fantastic interiors for their habitations, and his drowsiness, no friend to ingenuity, endowed them with increasingly anthropopathic features, for which reason they remained uninhabited. Imperceptibly skewed by sleep, his legally conscious consciousness even articulated complaints about them as though they were rowdy neighbors: "What the devil are they doing, carrying on like that," he grumbled, "Partying? making love, having dinner or what?"

The official version of the wasps' world order could be observed in the daytime. As if directed by an experienced air traffic controller and maintaining a strict order and rhythm, some insects flew out of the nest while others came in to land, carrying food, booty and goods of various kinds. It all seemed more or less understandable. You could even read about it in books. Order hymenoptera (membrane-winged), sub-order apocrita (stemlike), superfamily vespoidea (wasplike). Fine, but what is the meaning of that nocturnal droning—dz-z-z-hu-u-u-shrkh-okh-kh—that sounds like some unreal transformer?

As a rule, acoustics can also become a source of fear.

No, of course you didn't react to otherworldly voices, or screams from beyond the wall, or the creak of bolts and shutters. The cheap Hollywood repertoire could do no more than pleasantly tickle your nerves. But as soon as night came and you closed your eyelids, your ineffable "I," which until then had been delimited by the surface of your body, immediately migrated inward, to the inside of that imaginary membrane, and as sleep advanced, reconquering ever broader territories (much as, in a palace where there are hundreds of wide-open doors and the rooms stretch along the perspective of an immensely long corridor, the lights go out one at a time, beginning with the most distant chambers), so your light-loving "I" retreated and became localized. You felt yourself become progressively smaller and smaller, tinier—tiny—very tiny, compact, your inner vision (a victim of lagophthalmia) easily penetrated into the microworld, and "you" yourself now belonged to the microworld and were located somewhere in the region of the dream artery, and suddenly the pulsations of this artery, pulsations that you had entirely forgotten and that now took on for you in your shrunken state the dimensions of an earthquake, flung you up to the surface of your sleep together with the crumpled debris of the metaphorical castle, and the scarcely perceptible friction between your epithelium and your pillow slip was transformed into the grating and crashing of a natural disaster.

Sometimes a detail—a rattling noise in your knapsack that had not been there before—put you in fear of possible pursuit. You redoubled your pace, looking over your shoulder repeatedly, changing direction unexpectedly, diving into gateways. On rounding a corner you would turn sharply on your heel and head back, hoping to discover your invisible stalker, but all these stratagems, borrowed from spy films, proved fruitless; the pursuer's pounding gait constantly gained on you, your personal monster was already breathing down your neck, ready to devour you or tear you to pieces, until suddenly everything was explained: exhausted by running, bathed in sweat and angry at yourself, you finally realized that the cause of that unaccustomed sound effect was merely the accidental and unique juxtaposition of things, surfaces and textures in your knapsack.

Sometimes what troubled you was uncertainty about where a sound came from. After lunch one day you wasted a lot of time and turned the kitchen upside down before you worked out that an unrepeatable melodious whistle came from an ordinary saucepan of warm soup sucking in air as it cooled. The secret lay in the saucepan's lid, which sealed the vessel almost hermetically and served as the resonator in this culinary harmonium.

But enough, my dear fellow! Enough! There is only so much respect that you can pay the ingenious Morpheus and his trickster friends. There is only so much reflection that you can do. It is time for life and action!

Already one can hear the tedious twang of the turtledove and her partner's sharp unpleasant cackle as he informs her of his return.

Already the cleaner's broom is scratching the asphalt (it's that woman alcoholic from next door; like you, she lives by the holy spirit of the full goblet; they found her son dead a year ago in the entrance hall and the whole building heaved a sigh of relief, he'd got everyone's back up so much, that little bastard with the crooked legs and the hopeless collection of chromosomes).

Already the earliest of the local hygienists are beginning to shake out their rugs and runners (that sound has the uncanny property of echoing from the walls in such a way that the whipcracks keep on resonating long after the hygiene freak has finally retreated to his lair).

Already the first dogs of daylight are yelping hysterically, their owners' immature spoiled brats that they are. The night shift—the shaggy mongrel strays—have long ago barked their fill at the moon and had their way with their lady friends, and are now just getting ready for sleep atop the warm covers of sewer manholes, while their replacements rush out for a piss and gag on their idiotic barking as they greet a passing cyclist, an insistent fly or a sleepy sparrow.

Already beneath your balcony two women from neighboring apartments are quarreling over a clothesline, but really because one of them resents the new Mercedes that the other's husband enjoys driving up to the entrance, blowing the horn at length to signal to his beloved.

Already some children, irrepressible in the early morning, scream like stuck pigs as they race a tin can around the yard—the one they were going to use a moment ago to play baker.

Already the motor of the garbage truck is growling outside your window—a bit loud for such an old nag, or maybe they're digging up the road in quest of a water main that is probably mythical, but in any case ruptured.

So rise, draw your curtains aside. You haven't forgotten? Coming down. Dawn. Day.

The Story of Wozzeck

Well then, now that everything has been drawn aside, including the curtains, you need to do something. With yourself. With your memory of A. And with Wozzeck.

In the light of day the details of your descent wane, but your obligations are all the more clearly visible. And so, bearing in mind the need to be answerable for your words—oh yes, bearing that very firmly in mind!—you set about recreating Wozzeck's destiny, which brought him in the end to a white room with a barred window, a bed, etc., a tiny room recognizable to all as a ward in a lunatic asylum.

About a year or a year and a half earlier, having returned from one of the business trips that he so dreaded (largely because of his existential angst at the thought of railway stations and, even more, because you-he-I could not get used to a state of affairs where, trapped in a metal box—and what are railway carriages, aircraft cabins, cars and ships if not metal boxes?—with other slaves, you had to pretend that everything was fine, under control, you were simply on a trip. While the engine drones smoothly on or, say, the clatter of wheels on rails lulls you to sleep, you can accept the rules of the game and tolerate this limited space, this proximity of strangers, these unfamiliar smells and this infernal light, but the moment the train makes a longer stop at some midnight siding, the hellish silence, diluted by snoring from the top bunk and a child's whimpering in the neighboring compartment, forces you to leap to your feet and seek solace either in a stinking cigarette at the end of the carriage or in the remnants of the home-cured ham that you devour in a panic), well then, having returned from a business trip, here is what Wozzeck did: he disconnected the phone, cut the radio wire, threw out the antenna and the television set, took all his books, his radio receiver, tape recorder, audio system, cassettes, records, etc. to the garage (the garage, a part of his inherited estate, was empty) and, last of all, locked his wife and son in the basement of his apartment building. This would not have been so bad, except that he kept them there (feeding them, naturally, and carrying out their wastes) for a few hours short of three hundred thirty-three days, at which point the prisoners were rescued by municipal police acting on information from concerned neighbors who suspected foul play, kept a watchful brief, put two and two together, and let the cat out of the bag. Throughout this time Wozzeck assiduously attended his workplace (he was employed by a grubby little paper that ministered to the intellectual needs both of housewives and of sentimental overripe maidens), and in the evenings he regularly patronized the Dewdrop Cafe, where he just as regularly got drunk. His acquaintances began to shun the cafe to avoid being trapped by Wozzeck's inescapable tirades and his somewhat importunate alcoholic messianism. "Listen, old man," he usually began, leaning toward his interlocutor and plunging his elbow into a puddle of spilled coffee, damn, another stain, "Listen, old man, this world has lost its intimacy." Superficial or not, such a statement needed explaining, but logic always slipped out of Wozzeck's hands like a fish's tail and disappeared into the depths of his incoherence (objects and groups of objects, too, became slippery ichthyosauruses for him: exceed an agreed set—shoulder bag, wallet in the jacket, keys in the right-hand trouser pocket—and add, say, a scarf, gloves, passport, umbrella or airline ticket, and his life would turn into a hell of ceaseless stocktaking, a neurotic patting of pockets, rummaging in the briefcase, feeling the contents of suitcases, endlessly turning back and checking up, and all in vain, because in the end it was always the same: the umbrella sped away on the tram, the gloves stayed behind on a cafe table, the scarf in a cloakroom and the airline ticket, tucked into the passport (both expired) on a dresser in some antechamber; and so your scurrying between lost-luggage offices and check-in counters appears to be an absolutely superfluous epilogue: the plane taxis toward the runway, the staff shrug solicitously, and the treacherous objects complete another desertion), while the unfortunate listener was inundated with a kind of incomprehensible gruel containing everything—politics, video clips, Catholicism, advertisements for tampons, Hollywood, the media, computers, condoms, hit parades, porno films, fashion, and Lord knows what else. Wozzeck knew he was not being very convincing, so he would pull faces, correct himself, rub his forehead, knead his chin and furiously poke his nose—things he never allowed himself to do when sober. The point of all his pathos boiled down to the rejection of generally accepted cultural values, such as art or democracy or scientific and technological progress. The so-called joy of life, deemed "so-called" by Wozzeck himself, came in for especially harsh treatment. "As for this much-vaunted so-called joy of life of yours," he would say, "e.g., summer in Hawaii, an evening on Broadway, skateboarding in Florida, surfing in the Bahamas, the festival in Cannes, a weekend in Disneyland...what else? skiing in the Carpathians, love in Paris, bordellos in Amsterdam, beer in Bavaria, hockey in Canada, reggae in Jamaica, roulette in Monte Carlo, skyscrapers in New York, cigars in Cuba, war in Yugoslavia, gold in Alaska, hunting in Africa, emigrants at Brighton Beach, terrorists in Palestine, nirvana in India, oil in the Emirates, art in Montmartre, gauguin in Tahiti, rock in Woodstock, harakiri in Kyoto, carnival in Brazil, healing in Lourdes, the gioconda at the Louvre, death in Venice,[52] the bazaar in Chernivtsi,[53] corruption in High Places, a bullfight in Toledo, a miracle in Milan, an inferno in the Tower,[54] the pope in the Vatican, the tower in Babel, the bomb in Hiroshima, the rhumba in Barbados, a caravan in the Desert, the queen in England, a sauna in Finland, lenin in the Mausoleum, shadows in Paradise,[55] the sarcophagus in Chornobyl, can-can in the Moulin Rouge, cheese in Butter, a bird in the Hand, two in the Bush, lucy in the Sky,[56] islands in the Stream,[57] alice in Wonderland, fool on the Hill, in Vino veritas, the festival-that-is-always-with-you[58]—it's all sin and sodomy and the devil. Yes or no?" After any such absurd-yet-brilliant improvisation Wozzeck would solemnly pronounce that happiness was a condition approached only after experiencing fear, humility, contrition and despair. Here he would again make a disgruntled pause, detecting in these words a sour note of sectarianism, and to camouflage this he would begin feverishly persuading his listener that one should outlaw the press ("So what if I work for a newspaper?"), television and the Internet, place quotas on any kind of information, introduce merciless censorship and global information taxes and, most importantly, seal all international borders. ("And after that pray,

pray, pray—how and for what?—for the salvation of the soul.") Naturally, few people endured to the end of this gibberish.

And yet, dedicating his evenings to talk and drink, Wozzeck was not simply killing time. His sermon, though demented and incoherent, gradually matured, grew in stylistic polish, acquired a patina of imagery and sprouted woolly metaphors and juicy details. He knew it almost by heart, tested the effect of this or that innovation on his audiences and labored diligently to perfect the verbal construction that in his mind was beginning to resemble a flight of architectural fancy: thin supports on either side, a triumphal arch on top, and empty space in the middle.

For Wozzeck was training for a mission far more ambitious than the conversion of local drunks.

He intended, as soon as the text of his epistle approached not so much any ideal form as his vision of architectural and archlike completeness, to walk out onto the central square of the city (having previously freed his family from the basement), climb the equestrian statue of Marcus Aurelius[59] and proclaim his final announcement, his prophecy, his Revelation of Wozzeck.

And then, unheard, possibly derided, possibly ignored, he would descend (that is, come down), douse himself with gasoline and end his life on the sinful pyre of self-immolation.

So the timely intervention of the municipal police simultaneously saved three lives. To be sure, Wozzeck believed that only by imprisoning his family in the basement—an illegal act in the opinion of the authorities—could he protect his son and his wife from the menace of a decadent, evil, lascivious world; and although psychiatrists are still unsure how convinced he was of this claim, one can concur that he loved them—his son and his wife. He loved his son. He loved his wife.

And yet, as the beloved *Großmeister* would have said, "his heart belonged to another woman."[60]

The Story of A.

Well, what can you say about A.? She was so...so... You never even knew exactly how to describe the color of her hair until you read something that might have been written especially about her:

"gracefully bearing her basket, a woman with hair the shade of honey and the name of a Spartan crosses the square."[61]

For you the story of A. belongs to the same category as the reburial of relics (Where should they go? To their homeland?). And yet, and yet.

Her father was a well-known personality, the administrator of the famous Circus Vagabundo[62] and also, as was usual, a party boss and an informer. The circus often toured abroad, and the regime needed one of its own in that position. Naturally, laboring in the very furnace of the entertainment factory, he found it impossible to maintain an ascetic lifestyle. He had not only to employ girl acrobats, dancers, tight-rope walkers and chaste lady sword-swallowers, cultivate flautists in the women's orchestra, exercise guardianship over masochistic assistants whom insatiable magicians often and mercilessly sawed in two, but also to look after a famous dynasty of animal tamers (at a gesture of the beauteous Miriam's hand, tigers fell to the ground, rolled over like kittens, and then came the unforgettable scene: she majestically stretched herself out upon them as if they were striped rugs). There were temptations every step of the way, you'll agree. He made no effort to avoid them. His wife, of course, guessed that her dearly beloved engaged regularly in such salto mortales but said nothing until the notorious scandal of his open and turbulent affair with a certain Gertrud Boddenwier[63] (her posters read:

Queen Margot.[64]
Unsurpassed
Serpent-woman). Suddenly infatuated with the inexhaustible possibilities that her plasticity opened up in bed, he threw caution to the winds, almost losing his job and the favor of the bosses. A person of his rank, naturally, had the right to a mistress but not to a divorce. "I'll have your party card, you prick!" the first secretary of the district committee had yelled. Somehow they managed to hush up the affair, but his wife proved implacable. They did not formally divorce, but from then on he had to live apart from her.

And yet, A. (at the mention of her father, her mother would close up and go silent) often dropped into the Vagabundo after school. Not so much to collect her father's generous guilt-swollen gifts as to walk the circus corridors, linger in the wardrobe and rub shoulders with the garrulous, piebald and picturesque circus crowd. She liked to sit high up on the trapeze supports or on the orchestra platform and watch the rehearsals; she loved the smells of the arena, the spicy aroma of the makeup rooms and the stench of the animal stalls. She rejoiced in the movement, the spirit, the commotion, the noise, the colors, the glitter. Here she first saw real work—work to the seventh sweat, to the point of exhaustion—and understood the meaning of perfection: the importance of every millimeter of distance, every gram of weight, every twitch of the muscles.

On finishing school she enrolled in the university's journalism faculty but kept up her old habit of visiting the circus. Even her first press report was dedicated to the Vagabundo: a short note and an unrepeatable photograph only slightly spoiled by shabby printing: trapeze artists captured in flight, under the very top of the cupola (she herself had thought up this ingenious camera angle) at the instant when their bodies formed the mysterious Chang pictogram.

(Perhaps it is just such signs that we should try to decode. Each of us. For they are prompts from an invisible prompter. Listen and look!)

So it was entirely to be expected that A. encountered her first love in the circus. He was the scion of yet another eminent circus family—a dynasty of jugglers, acrobats and equilibrists, the Mokhóis. The patriarchs of this clan had entertained carnival crowds in the town squares of the Middle Ages, belching flames in the shadows of churches, juggling torches, erecting human pyramids. Over seven centuries the clan mixed with its own the blood of the most varied origins—Saxon and Gypsy, Jewish and Basque, Sicilian and Magyar. Even a Moor attached himself to the itinerant family; wholly undistinguished, already in the second generation he was justly forgotten by his relatives, so that when his great-great-great-great-granddaughter bore her blue-eyed husband a Negro child, nobody could think of any explanation save adultery, and nobody rescued the innocent woman from an undue death: the imaginary cuckold killed his wife together with the infant. As late as the beginning of the century the family still wandered the roads of Europe. Finally the universal passport law pinned it down somewhere near Odesa. It was the age of great cataclysms, of a world split into two; ships no longer sailed for Constantinople, that's how it was.

This youngest of the Mokhóis was talented. From the age of fifteen he performed his own solo number and was described in the program notes as an "artist working in an original genre." What was original about the show was that the youth, while situated atop an immensely tall pole, which in turn rested on a sphere, which for its part wobbled on a cylinder, which swayed on the spike of a cone that, finally, stood on a unstable bowlegged table—the youth, located atop this less than reliable construction, performed such acrobatic contortions as throwing his legs over his shoulders, standing on his head and weaving his limbs into various ingenious knots. In addition to these talents he was endowed with a cheerful disposition, a quick mind and a sharp tongue.

A. fell madly in love with him.

Nothing is worse than a belated first love. It always seems final and real, real and final. But that's by the by.

Her state of bliss lasted almost a year, until the youthful Mokhói failed to return from a foreign tour. Or rather, it was not that he failed to return but that he remained abroad, and not just anywhere, but in that Mecca of every circus artist, the Principality of Monaco. His performance at the world festival of circuses appealed so greatly to the prince of this tiny country that in contravention of all regulations and quotas and provisions and determinations and instructions the scion of the ancient line of comedians was granted citizenship.

But that was not the worst blow. For it turned out that for the entire year during which he happily loved A., our hero also nurtured his very own fiancée, who at the time of his acquiring the Monaco passport was already in the ninth month of pregnancy; as a result, the population of the Mediterranean principality increased all at once by three.

For several months after these tidings A. was as if stunned. She did not leave home, mostly she said nothing (her mother tried not to disturb her without urgent cause), said nothing and wept and, refusing to dry her tears, watched through a veil of damp despair telecasts of the Monte Carlo world festival of circuses where, under the gaze of a huge crowd and disguised as a red joker, her only love gyrated atop a tall pole.

One year later,

not even a cinematographic year, but the kind of кінематographic subtitled year after which, unrecognized, the stepdaughter returns to the land of her birth as the wife of a millionaire; the millionaire (who is also a count), it transpires, is the demobilized soldier who suffers from amnesia and whose memory returns thanks to this neurophysiological Cinderella. He ultimately marries yet another flesh and blood Cinderella—a blind flower girl who, naturally, is miraculously cured before the finale; and in the end the twin brothers meet. The one, kidnapped in childhood, has become a noble villain, the other—the rich Maecenas whom the former unwittingly robs. Thus, too, A.'s meeting with Wozzeck was probably the dramatic end—one year later—of somebody else's film, though at first it looked like an intriguing prologue.

There is no need to describe their summer or, more precisely, the not quite two months that in the herbariums of memory bear the title of the Summer of the Infinite Indulgence of Time, for Time transformed these fifty-two sunny days into fifty-two sunny years (clarinets).[65] And today, how pallid seem the collections of other years next to those colorful, fragrant, crisp manifestations of the Summer summer

(*long ago it was Summer summer, but now it is winter*):

—those thickets of jointweed, impossible in the endlessness of their expanse; when you lie among them, screwing up your eyes skyward, they resemble microscopic conifers, but in the real forest the bushes of jointweed are different, in the forest jointweed dares not play at imitation in the presence of real pines and spruces and drops its epaulettes in feigned resignation;

—thick ferns that resemble the archaeopteryx fossil whose picture in a school textbook has pursued you all your life; among those ferns you came across a cool, shady spring and wanted to wash your sweaty faces but had to run away because of the myriad mosquitoes and her allergy to fern spores;

—a giddyingly sweet-smelling linden tree in somebody's yard; you drank wine beneath its branches, ignoring the eloquent disapproval in the looks of the hostile aborigines, you drank wine and kissed, and the linden drowned in its own languor and, saturated with sap and the murmur of bees, shed droplets of a sweet honey rain like a candle;

—a field of pea and lentil, so comforting and colorful from afar, yet dry and uneven to the touch, its soil ploughed by tractor. You dared not even cross the strip abutting the field (it was like the no-man's-land alongside a state border), inhabited by a cosmopolitan rabble of couch grass, plantain, clover, knotgrass, chamomile, goosefoot, marjoram, wormwood, coltsfoot, sow thistle, thistle and burdock;

—overripe cherries, beginning to wither on one side (she loved that slightly bitter aristocratic taste of decadence in berries), red currants, blueberries, blackberries that turned your lips purple like the exhausting kisses of your youth, it was only the gooseberries that you left alone, repelled by the greenish fruit with its indecent veins that reminded you of the aged and half-blind eyes of rough-skinned reptiles;

—magnificent as an orchid, the flower of the pumpkin on its thick spiky stem; one day he ceremoniously presented her with such a flower, forgetting what it means to "hand someone a pumpkin."[66] He remembered only later, in the autumn, after her devastating departure, as he devoured implausible quantities of pumpkin porridge with the most varied sauces imaginable (what a counterattack by vengeful fate!). He did not even manage a bitter smile but went on silently gorging on the sweetish fare, perhaps taking vengeance on the treacherous vegetable, perhaps attempting some kind of record-breaking pumpkin-eating suicide;

—and, of course, mistletoe, mistletoe, mistletoe, whose round bushes stood like milestones along the routes of your summer journeys (the poplars on either side of the road, half their branches dead, had long ago pawned their leaves to the enterprising mistletoe and were now wearing out these clothes from the usurer's back), it was mistletoe that, strictly speaking, had started it all—those opulent white berries spilled on the bed in that little room (in the house next to the bridge). He had been lured there by a suspicious invitation, indestructible as a bad penny, and there he met her, the woman *with hair the shade of honey and the name of a Spartan.*

For A. this was a summer of melting, of thawing out from a deathly cold spell. That summer for the first time she released herself from her oath of sorrow, discovering with childish surprise that during her absence the world had not died, nor disappeared, nor collapsed in shame at its own imperfection, and night followed day as before, and the sun had not begun to rise in the west, and the third part of the rivers was not made bitter.[67] And that after the time of the stinging pain, when she thought she had neither strength nor will nor desire to breathe, it was possible, after all, to rejoice in the ending of the day and the midnight downpour that washes away in a moment the remains of the day's heat, capturing streets and city blocks with its sudden energetic sibilance, catching the city in a ring of cheerful sparkling electricity (there are flashes on the wet asphalt of the neighborhood fire department, on the dark glass of garage doors, on the glistening sides of crimson oil trucks—vessels for a temporarily uninteresting fluid), and from all sides echoes triumphal thunder, beating with aboriginal enthusiasm upon invisible tom-toms, drums, kettledrums and giant gongs that fail to withstand these blows and shatter, and the nearby membranes of windows shudder (the ecumenical broad-mindedness of the celestial percussionists is such that the curly-haired Zeus beats the bongos, the Vedic Indra prances by with a tambourine, the macaronic Jupiter works the maracas, the Finn Ukko clicks the castanets, Perun of the Slavs refrains from his customary farting and rattles his scrotum instead, and Balu (Beelzebub) teases the marimba); it was possible after a storm to enjoy the transparency of the air that comes in from outside and that on the other side of the curtain fills the night with its immanent incandescence, its St. Elmo's fires, its neon, ozone, cesium, uranium, its polar lights, its ball lightning, its ballpoint pens, its magnetic fields, its magnetos, its photons and flash photography, and from this eddy of light a lake is born, cloudy as ancient silver, its surface veiled in mist, a lake in the forest before dawn, and she disrobes—the mist at once enshrouds the garments cast upon the ground—and steps into its quiet milky waters, these waters support her as easily as the dense waters of the Dead Sea, formed as it was from tears, a light movement of the hand is enough to set you gliding across the silent surface, you float, you fly, you speed with implausible velocity, reach the opposite shore, then just as easily return, and then again, and again, and your body rejoices and luxuriates in the soft embrace, and you understand that you are free to spin and turn and go up and down because the dimensions here are different, and gravity is but a projection of your desires, this is your world, certainly real, not invented, and you are free in it, free everywhere, finally free, freeforevermore...—breathless, happy, relaxed, she has woken up, and the late sun of the forenoon that here in the room has warmed her face—there are even beads of sweat on the bridge of her nose—has already dried the asphalt outside, and therefore a new life is beginning, and all routes lead to the building next to the railway bridge where each of you shall discover what he or she deserves: some a way out, others a cul-de-sac.

52 days, 51 nights

And so, late one sunny morning she walked out into the street with the feeling that the past was finished, a new life was beginning, and this very day something would finally happen. In the course of a year she had forgotten nothing, of course, but the dark crevice in her memory had become so much a part of her that, willing or not, she made peace with it as you make peace with the existence of your base physiological self. In her handbag, as well as a comb, a pouch decorated with beads that served as a purse (a tribute to past hippie sympathies) and a half-eaten apple, there was an invitation to an exhibition, rolled into a tube and secured with an elastic headband. She had simply not bothered to throw it out the previous week, but today, little by little, it gathered meaning as a pass into the realm of freedom (what a paradoxical phrase, when you think of it—a *realm of freedom*). The city, washed overnight, was lazily taking pleasure in the summer's day. The green—copper oxide? chromium oxide?—"cupola of the corner building, like a warrior's helmet,"[68] a church, a shaded street with a phone booth and carbonated water dispenser, a square, a fountain, pigeons, Marcus Aurelius's horse (*Bolivar cannot carry double*)[69] and Aurelius himself with brown streaks down his impassive face, endless marble stairs leading ever upward to the local Olympus with the massive bulk of the Vagabundo looming on top (in the course of a year the circus had greatly deteriorated, the troupe had all but broken up and the best artists were seeking their fortunes in capital cities elsewhere. Mokhói proved light-fingered (or, rather, fleet-footed), the cashbox empty, and the city learned with something approaching communal grief of the death of its favorite, the python Papathanasio (Pants in common parlance), about whom it was rumored that for a bet he would satisfy the most insolent demands of his lady trainer; so now A.'s daddy, that old Zhivago,[70] busied himself with refurbishing the arena for rock concert crowds), but that is not our route, we continue down the maple-lined avenue past the theater to the bridge where trains labor to gather speed and display in their windows an itinerant gallery of human folly (and at each end of each carriage the first enthusiasts stand watch, waiting for the attendant to open the yearned-for WC).

She walked beautifully. Even if you were to look down from above at a crowd of thousands, in that sea of brownian head-wagging you would recognize at once her light, supple and gracious movements. Waiting for her of a morning in the open-air cafes of summer, permitting himself neither coffee, nor cigarettes, nor wine just yet, Wozzeck would notice from afar her bright dress, generously billowed by a wind that had fallen head over ears in love, he would recognize her downy hair blown in all directions, and the uncommon gait that giddied him and made his heart stand still, and something would happen inside him that resembled an avalanche of bankrupt organs.

Like everyone with allergic reactions, she had thin, sensitive skin, and it was of many priceless shades—different on her face, her neck (he would bend over to kiss her delicate ear, plunge his face into the fragrant intoxicating hair, descend to where it gave way to a fine down, and even further to the soft yielding back, and further still, further still—that will do, impertinent reader!), different again on the inside of the elbow and, most precious of all, iridescent like mother-of-pearl, on the wrist. He discovered many favorite nooks, but with time grew stronger in the belief that he loved every part of her—even the fold that promised to thicken as the years passed by, the web of blood vessels that would swell with the birth of a child, and the out-of-place birthmark (as soon as they embraced, it stopped being out of place and became part of a harmonious symmetry, for he had one that was exactly the same). All his previous notions of Hellenic and *Vogue*ish perfection melted like the impure dream of some pimply oaf—for here was she, the most beautiful, the most perfect, the most desired!

If one believes Cortázar, the outlines of her fine mouth bore witness to petty cruelty, and perhaps for that reason, when she found herself in front of a mirror, she would lift her upper lip ever so slightly and immediately become so helpless—idiot Cortázar!—that you simply swooned with tenderness and pain and rushed to kiss her beloved fine-ever-so-fine-finest-in-the-world mouth, her beautiful eyes and her delicate hands. And so, when she glanced in passing at a mirror behind the bar of a certain pub, this led naturally to a curious event: in an ecstasy of feelings you spilled the coffee, knocked a plate from the table and upended the sugar bowl. "Fortunately it is sugar, not salt,"[71] said a bald and disreputable-looking old codger in Russian, dusting off his trousers. And, with a snap of his false teeth, he introduced himself: "Timofei Pahlch, Prah-fessr."[72] (They both had to shake the professor's hand, and despite his confusion and embarrassment Wozzeck felt a jab of primeval envy as the birdlike professorial claw clutched her narrow, elegant palm. Women's hands, in contrast to men's, generally differ very little from one another: a little larger, a little smaller, prettier, uglier—they are all of a kind. Perhaps the most primitive of them, and the most deserving of a place in the collector's cabinet, are the hands of lady typesetters, trade-union treasurers and proofreaders of local newspapers with their incipiently degenerate fingernails. The perfection and uniqueness of A.'s wrist testified to evolution's centuries-long experiments with the blood of emperors and queens, of their lovers and favorites, of plotters, regicides, adventurers and insolent servants).

She would come in the morning, usually on the way back from tennis, waving her racquet from afar. He would kiss her salty shoulder, bring coffee, look, listen and inhale. That is how their day began. At first she talked a lot. About everything—her father, Vagabundo, the family quarrels (a plate shatters on the checkerboard floor), about school (that poultry yard where every protagonist felt like an ugly duckling), about university (her first rock, her first sex, her first high), about the young Mokhói (her inner gaze habitually worked its way upward: table, cone, cylinder, sphere, pole, the man himself), about her love of photography, about loneliness, about wanting to travel and study, about loneliness, about her favorite music, about loneliness, about her plans, about loneliness, about journalism, about loneliness, about...

For her this summer became a season of talking it through, of revising a lesson she had shed tears over. It was as if to enter her new life she had to pass an exam that was half from boarding school and half from Freud.

Wozzeck prepared for these meetings with the obsessive diligence of a hygienist. He woke up five hours early. Certain of not getting back to sleep, he got up, did a few half-hearted exercises, showered, consuming in one session three days' supply of soap and water, shaved, then spent a long time dressing (neither before nor afterwards did he pay any attention to clothes), undressing and dressing again, gyrated in front of the mirror like the dottiest of nitwits (to put it very, very mildly), employed a multitude of secret devices (most likely pinched from the arsenal of expensive prostitutes) to check that everywhere he was clean and shiny, and finally, long before the appointed hour, emerged from the house. At first he took his bicycle (he lived on the outskirts and had to traverse a good half of the city), but fate found the besotted mammale's descent into imbecility so hilarious that it had no choice but to put spokes in his wheel, even if they were only metaphysical:

One day they had agreed to meet later than usual—at noon. He woke up as always when it was still pitch dark, performed all of his mating rituals and, as there was still plenty of time, he did the shopping, tidied the house (even cleaning the cobwebs from the ceiling, something that did not pass without anatomical damage: he bruised his elbow and broke the last remaining ear from his china candleholder), had another shower and set off on his joyous *bicycle race*.[73] But the sun had already warmed the streets, the cobblestones glimmered with heat, and soon he was perspiring. At midway he turned back, got under the shower again, changed into dry clothes and resolved to stay fresh by riding slowly on the shady side of the streets. The trouble was that around midday the shadows had already curled up into tight little rolls and pressed themselves against the buildings; he had to swerve to avoid protruding stairs, storm-water pipes and grapevines, he grazed his knees against the walls and was obliged to brake at each corner, carefully descend to the road and almost immediately bring the bicycle up on its haunches again to leap onto the next sidewalk. It was like riding some mentally deficient bowlegged nag or Munchhausen's mare with its arse whittled away[74] by some *Easy Rider's* axe.[75] In five minutes Wozzeck was in a lather worthy of a centaur, so he went back again. He took yet another shower, the day's fourth, changed his linen and appeared on the street as a neat pedestrian who strolled toward the city center without haste, avoiding *sunshine spots* and extolling the virtues of walking. Even the sickly breeze in his face—the hygienist's joy—welcomed this Solomonic-Wozzeckian resolution, but together with physical relief it also carried the sound of distant chimes from the city hall clock tower: a quarter to twelve. Wozzeck is seized by a light panic: he suddenly realizes that even by sprinting he cannot save himself from being late. Cursing the weather and his own idiocy, he rushes headlong for home and his bicycle, but here he encounters another twist: there is no water. Evidently his carefree bathing has transgressed all imaginable transcendental norms. On the other hand, as we shall see, fate's rational miserliness was quite justified: *Bi-i-i-icycle!*

Bi-i-i-i-icycle!

Bicycle, bicycle, bicycle, bicycle-e-e-e race!

Anyone who happened to be on the street at this time would have witnessed an unrepeatable spectacle: the shadow of a frenzied cyclist flitting wavelike over the convexities of the street cobbles, and above the shadow, aglimmer with spokes and sandal buckles, a racing futurist hybrid with the head of a record breaker and a mechanical body. *We are the champions*, mate, *we are the champions*.[76] But there was nobody under the linden trees and nobody in the tree-lined avenue.

There is probably no need to say how Wozzeck, sweat-drenched and miserable, arrived one and a half minutes late and did not find A. at the appointed place, and how he was seized by panic, even though he knew that she was usually ten or fifteen minutes late, and how his fear turned into deathly despair after these fifteen or twenty or twenty-five minutes passed without result—cold sweat came on top of hot—and how it was only an hour later that he got up the courage to phone and found out from her mother that she had a temperature and a cruel bout of tonsillitis induced, no doubt, by yesterday's excessively chilled 1989 sauvignon blanc.

The Dream of Coming Late

But at least once I really was late (she seized on this with relief as justification of her coolness) after shamefully sleeping in. Oddly enough, my dream on that occasion was dedicated to the theme of lateness.

The scene of the action was a department store where Anton had once worked as manager[77] (he now has a shop of his own opposite the theater, a visit to which was to be part of the dream—Anton had bought the tickets). I was sitting with three of his friends in a storeroom filled to overflowing with goods (the quantity was not immediately obvious—the niches of the dream world are always conjectural until the eye focuses on them). Anton himself had disappeared somewhere, busy as always, but he had given his managerial sanction to the consumption of a bottle of cognac. "Drink it up, folks, don't be shy, it'll improve the quality of the show." But because we did not know one another, and because the bottles of cognac were not simply stored in boxes but packed in festive sets that included chocolates, New Year decorations and champagne, and you could only get to them by untying a colored ribbon, tearing open some shiny metal foil—in a word, by spoiling a gift, it took a while before anyone would start. We sat in silence and smoked: a thickset redheaded fellow with psychoanalytic sideburns, a vaguely familiar short chap who might have been from another dream (that's right, he was the tiresome poet who wrote himself into his dreadful works as a mighty Saxon or a blond beast); and a subtle youth, not without his sublimations and with the profile of a Chopin. The smoke-diluted silence became unendurable, a provocation to indulge in loose and intemperate behavior (a familiar form of self-defense). Well, guys, are we going to put one down or what? They put one down. Things eased up a bit.

But other characters, attracted by the scent of cognac, swarmed into the plot. *Some Boborykin*[78] *or other* knocked at the door (it had been locked from inside) and by conjuring with Anton's name persuaded them to let him in and even pour him a shot. Other nameless ones pushed in. It got noisy and rowdy.

As I drank my cognac I was mindful of a chore that I had to perform. On the way to the theater I was to drop in on a company whose real-life prototype was Accord,[79] an advertising agency; in my dream I wrongly called it "Astock" (perhaps because a few years earlier there had been a firm of such a name, a competitor of Accord's). I had made an appointment for four in the afternoon so that I could easily get to the theater for the show at five. The nature of my business remained unclear, but I was sure that my contact was some mythical advertiser called *Vasia*.

Suddenly I realized that it was a quarter to four (although a moment ago it had been barely two), and I had to run, and the reason for this sharp leap in time, this compression of chronology, was the selfsame unpleasant Boborykin who had so rudely intruded on a company of strangers.

I ran out of the department store, the voiceless shadow of Anton accompanying me for a while, and ran along a tremendously long fence that I had never seen in the city before. Later I was able to place it—it was like the fence around the National Museum in Warsaw. Although the topography was local (if enriched with Warsaw features), the further I went the more certainly a different toponym emerged: Lviv. Yes, beyond all doubt, I was now in Lviv. And although the route I had in mind was still fairly authentic—up to the post office, then left along Sich Riflemen Street[80] to Accord, and then along Soviet Street to the theater—I already knew that this "up to the post office" could only be done on the Lviv Number 6 tram. The fence—the material embodiment of my lateness—refused to end and stretched to infinity, but time, collapsed by the coming of Boborykin, offered instantaneous climatic metamorphoses: as I ran out of the department store, summer was in full bloom; later, beyond the skeleton of the picket fence and against the museum walls I noticed the yellow carpet of November, and later still, running across the road on a red light, I unexpectedly plunged into a drift of thawing snow—not even winter snow, but the kind that resembles wisps of dirty cotton wool, snow of the first days of March (I wondered at the time why Anton was commercially so inept as to stock out-of-date New Year's gifts—remember the cognac?). At that crossing I was almost run over by a vehicle, an ugly green oil truck, for at the very last moment, when I already had one foot on the sidewalk, it turned out that to make my progress more difficult (you know that dream sensation of running, but in hopelessly slow motion?)

I had been burdened with a huge trolley laden with suitcases and cartons—I barely managed to haul it up onto the sidewalk. With that trolley (which grew ever larger and heavier, finally turning into an overloaded trailer) I barely crawled, a miserable rickshaw coolie, squelching the melting snow under my feet. I had no idea where the yearned-for stop of the Number 6 tram might be. It was almost four. It would have been good at least to call and warn the mythical Vasia that I would be late. But the nearest phone booth was in use, and I did not want to stop and wait: it seemed to be one of my hated classmates phoning. Looking for another telephone, I dived into a gateway—literally "dived," because at that moment my luggage had grown so large that it became a powerful truck, but the truck was at the other end of a drive-through courtyard under whose exit arch stood three men.

Perhaps there is a case for slowing down and resting, because all these metamorphoses make one's head spin.

So under the arch there were three men. Dressed in military coats, they cast a hostile look in my direction, and I realized that they were hostile because I was in a sergeant's uniform and my truck was a military vehicle. I vaguely remembered two of them from somewhere, but the third I knew—we had studied together at the institute (in one group, by the way, with the aforementioned Sasha Abramian; this fellow was also called Sashko, but his surname had got lost in the sclerotic maze of my memory). They stood around aimlessly under the arch, smoking, and the only reason they did not salute me, a sergeant, was that today was Constitution Day, and they were entitled to a holiday, a twenty-four-hour release from duty. I wanted to pass by without even greeting Sashko, but as I came through the archway I saw between me and the road where my truck was parked a strip of military territory cordoned off with barbed wire, and then a railway line. It was impossible to get across, so, willing or not, I had to ask the way.

While I was still in the clutches of this outrageously surreal dream, quizzing surly soldiers about the way to the tramline that would be my guide—for now that I had transport of my own, I had no need of the tram itself—she, my beloved, had probably returned from her tennis and was sitting at a cafe table, waiting for her lie-abed, her ne'er-do-well, glancing impatiently at her watch and plotting a future *amazing case of a woman's revenge*. But this was taking place in a world to which I was not destined to return just yet. I still had not given up hope of phoning Accord and telling them I was running late. There was a telephone in some office jam-packed with stuff—an insurance office or something. I could barely push my way among the tables, and the tables were heaped with dusty ledgers, accounts and rolls of calculations. There was a queue for the phone, and while I searched in my notebook for Accord's number, an inquisitive lady standing in the line asked whether she could see my collection of business cards. For some unknown reason I yielded to her frankly impudent request. Finally I was on the line to the invisible subscriber, and an unfamiliar voice told me that Vasia, unfortunately, could not come to the phone, though he was actually around and would be for a while yet, so he would get my message about my unintentional and exhausting delay, except that unfortunately it was quite impossible to call him to the phone because in the next room all the Accord staff were intently watching the television coverage of the European football championship. So that was that. As I listened to these ravings, bereft of style and taste, even the style and taste of dreams, I kept one eye on the old lady and was now convinced that my imagination was quite out of control, for my business card collection had transformed itself in the stranger's hands (so easily that I knew I was being mocked with impunity) into an album of school photographs, and inquisitive insurance officers were already leafing through it. I ended up as one of their number, straining on tiptoe and peering over shoulders in an effort to see. And as soon as I caught sight of a photo of that detested classmate whose presence in the phone booth on the street I had found so intolerable, I woke up, realizing haplessly and helplessly that today's meeting with the beloved would not take place.

52 days, 51 nights

In those days A. felt as if she had walked out into the open for the first time after a long and severe illness, she had forgotten how it was done and was losing her balance, and somebody was supporting her and helping her take the first step—here's an arm, you can lean on it. After the shadows of the hospital ward, the light was so blinding that she could not tell whose arm it was.

As she got better, she was driven by a greedy enthusiasm to be everywhere, see everything, meet everyone, catch up on the whole lost year. There was no event in the city she did not want to attend. She rediscovered her journalistic streak, and everywhere she went she took along her powerful all-seeing Nikon, a gift from her father.

More and more, Wozzeck felt his desire to be with A. eclipse all his other wishes. Friends, work, habits, acquaintances, hobbies, duties all seemed petty, unnecessary and dull compared with the possibility of being with her. At first he was happy to accompany A. on her life-affirming excursions, but gradually the growing force of this colorful whirlpool began to annoy him, he felt it was superfluous, it took away precious time, minutes when they simply could be together.

It was not that A. was indifferent to Wozzeck's feelings, or even to Wozzeck himself. She even loved him, probably, and often made sacrifices for him, canceling plans and appointments. But now spending a whole evening at home seemed to her impossibly wasteful. That way you could miss out on everything in the world. They had different ideas about waste.

On one occasion he did not go to an event—a book launch or a concert—and stayed home, pleading a work deadline. Time passed, and she did not return. He prowled about the rooms. He listened at the door for the echo of her light steps and looked out the dark window, where he could see only his dim double, looking much more anxious than his real *vis-à-vis* in his own mind. Taking his shower, he repeatedly turned off the taps, fearing that he might miss the sound of the doorbell. She had a key, however. After all, human beings are born free, he told himself. That is even in the declaration of human rights. So be free. You should go to sleep. It's long after midnight. You simply have to go to sleep to prove to yourself and to her... What exactly he was going to prove remained unknown, but at last he drew a bath for her and went to bed. Perhaps he even slept, because the turning of the key in the lock came across as the continuation of a nightmare. She was softly singing to herself. She took of her shoes—a light tap—slipped on the security chain—a metallic clang—looked into the bathroom—a click of the switch and a creak of the door. There was some quiet laughter. Then she softly came into the room (infantile avenger that he was, he was breathing regularly and deeply, as though sound asleep), kissed him gently somewhere on his hair, dearest, she said, dearest, your girlfriend got shamelessly drunk without you. But you mustn't be angry with me. You're not angry, are you? Before she returned from the bathroom he was soundly and happily asleep. In the morning, waking up first, he watched her with a strange, pained tenderness as she slept, and thought: we'll be together. We'll always be together.

She loved him, she really did love him. But the youthful Mokhói's equilibrations had caused some little part of her heart to atrophy, and she was surprised to notice that, whereas in her circus youth nothing had meaning except mad all-consuming happiness—neither circumstance, nor place, nor company, nor surroundings, nor time—now any trifle could cause irritation: the knot of a tie, a turn of phrase, the color of the wallpaper, the chiming of a clock. Wozzeck demanded too much. He wanted to control every moment of her life. It was becoming burdensome. He was not jealous on account of her past, but the present had to belong wholly to him. It was only with difficulty now that he could avoid being possessive. He was becoming unbearable.

Nothing is worse than a belated first love. It always seems final and real, real and final. But that's by the by.

In time, things got worse. They began to argue. He threw fits of jealousy. She disappeared for long periods. Then she would come back, and in an access of emotion he would forgive everything, but he turned the act of forgiveness into a distasteful show of self-flagellation. After a few days of his pressing solicitude and his continuous, passionate, mindless and sheepish gaze, she wanted to escape to the ends of the earth, and she did escape. In short, this was a whole life. Who knows how it fitted into those fifty-two days and fifty-one nights.

On the morning of the fifty-second day he gave her his regular letter—they had a custom of writing to each other. Several years later the police found the draft of this letter during their search (a school notebook with a faded cover, the first page covered in flamboyant handwriting, and nothing else—emptiness, cleanliness, gridlines), and it was later bound together with other documents in the medical file. In the letter Wozzeck wrote the following:

"Only a little time has passed, and already I want to be with you again. It's so simple—to be with you. All the time, every moment of existence. I know nothing about love. Really. But I want to be with you. Every day to see you dress, comb your hair, sleep, eat, wash, pray, do things, or do nothing. To be alongside you. Next to you. No more. That's all.

I want to breathe the air that you breathe and the air that you exhale (that's probably a bit morbid, I agree).

I want to absorb all the scents of your body. They are beautiful. To kiss you everywhere that a mouth can reach. Endlessly to caress you. Feed you. Bathe you like a baby. Rock you to sleep. Be with you. Be you. Be.

I am jealous beyond belief. Of everything. Of the music you listen to without me, of the paintings you see by yourself, of books that I didn't give you to read. After all, I encompass the whole world. Everything you need. Everything. I cannot grasp how you manage to be somewhere outside me. How you manage to live apart. To have your own will. Desire something else. Breathe on your own.

What is it about the world that enchants you? What makes you want to travel? Where are the seeds of your temptations?

I am jealous for you. Hopelessly jealous. Jealous of the wine that makes you tipsy. Of the illnesses you suffer and the medicines that heal you. Of your hair that I don't control. Of your fingernails that grow of their own accord. Simply of you. This is very hard to explain. It's even more difficult to bear. I know that you, too, are tired. I've wronged you. It's been like a reign of terror. But there's nothing I can do. I want to possess you completely. I want to be with you.

I love you. I'm sorry if you don't like hearing this."

She did not read the letter straight away because she was off to another exhibition and needed to choose her dress, her hairdo and jewelry. She forgot about him and spent a lot of time in front of the mirror, inspecting herself from all sides, putting on now this, now that, childishly trying to imagine herself as different, modeling the shape of her mouth out of involuntary habit. Nothing brought him greater pleasure than contemplating these preparations of hers. She was neither one of those slightly built plain Janes nor a gaunt princess; her straight posture, the proportions of her body and her sense of space (space whose three-dimensional system of coordinates—x, y, z—reminded her of school; space through which she moved so perfectly and with such inborn decorum) suggested the subtlety and fragility of the most delicate of grasses. When she touched your body it was as though you had touched it yourself. She could read you more exactly than you could in your moments of greatest concentration. Her every movement, her every stance and involuntary gesture glowed with such perfect harmony that every attempt to describe them degenerated into raving and slobbering idolatry. But verily, verily I say unto you: there exist millions of tender creatures that nevertheless crash about in the world like a pestle in a mortar. Their step makes the earth shake. You are always bumping into their angular ribs and knees as though they were billiard tables, and their hands have all the sensitivity of a mechanical shovel.

She was...O God! She was...simply a woman fashioned from the astringent body of summer. A summer's body.

But she was getting dressed for the exhibition. It was the fifty-second and last day of their life together.

Bad luck often reads like the product of poor literary taste, and so what lay in wait for them was, once again, a building near the railway. Not, admittedly, the one where they had met—a different one across the bridge, large and white, with an imposing silver dome. They were the last to arrive. The public was already sidling furtively along walls hung full of canvases, artists were profoundly intoning "Om!" (having in mind, naturally, something quite other than a unit of electrical resistance),[81] the sound system alternately hissed and sputtered something suggesting Zen Buddhism, pungent Oriental incense sticks exuded sickly fumes through which cognoscenti battled to sniff the free-of-charge aromas of the anticipated refreshments, organizers were giving desperate interviews—in a word, everything was as usual. Everything was as usual, and therefore Borovchak and Schwarzkopf and Gorwitz and Nestor and Caesar and Putsyk with Yakovyna and Gustav & Gustav (of "Everything for Men" Co. Ltd.) had come, too.

In this atmosphere she felt like a fish in water. Many of her university friends were here, geniuses ready to take the first flight out, hirsute philosophers and gentrified poets. A special language, special customs and decorum held sway here. Quite different things were valued here than elsewhere, above all a herd instinct that they confused with membership of the elect.

For all her cunning, History has no record in her annals of the reason for, or rather the occasion of, the conflict. All of a sudden Wozzeck was seen to drag her roughly by the arm away from the crowd and say something to her, his face disfigured with anger. She was not tardy in replying. What she said must have hit home and stung, for almost simultaneously they turned their backs on each other and strode off in opposite directions, Wozzeck almost crashing his forehead into a wall. Then he knocked down somebody's painting and hung it back up, badly: it had fallen again before he took a single step away. He turned back involuntarily but gave up, ran down the stairs and stormed off.

Hearing laughter and commotion, she turned back but only saw two gangly youths trying to rehang a canvas that, she thought, must have fallen by accident.

Two days later, when she had read the letter and cooled down—she was quick to forget grievances—A. phoned Wozzeck. She thought they could make peace, as in the past. But he did not reply. Or rather, his reply was "no."

Stage Direction No. 1

The canvas that Wozzeck had knocked off the wall at the exhibition belonged to the brush, or rather Brush (for "belonged" suggests Brush with a capital "B," a lanky benefactor with five-o'clock shadow—let enthusiasts of pompous and vacuous terms like Love, Art and Eternity understand this as pompously and vacuously as they usually do) of one of the most interesting local painters, Matiash Kudusai. His attempts to break through to the pinnacles of art might strike some as dubious, but at least he was never short of imagination. It was he who, after the elapse of an indefinite quantity or expanse of this time of ours-and-yours, painted a portrait of A., but that was later, when A. had returned from her travels a famous person, almost a celebrity, having made herself a name (a name, a name, dear reader—the name we wrestle, you and I, so vainly to discover (here the desire to open parentheses arises anew, in order that one might picture this vain and vainglorious combat with the imaginary reader ("we wrestle, you and I"), but parentheses, unfortunately, create only the illusion that the text is three-dimensional, and no matter how many you insert one within the other, you will never achieve the effect familiar in the literature as "the Liubansky syndrome").

Stage Direction No. 2

Demonstrating the monstrous inertia of the machinery of love, the relationship between A. and Wozzeck continued for some time after the breakup, naturally enough, but it degenerated into a pathological frenzy of spying. They neither met nor talked but stalked each other like children, traced each other's new paths, worried about each other's new acquaintances and habits, greedily took in any talk or rumor about each other and sent each other cunningly camouflaged messages. To each other, each to the other, about each other.

But let them meet by chance in the city and fiendish pride hurls them asunder, and they race blindly apart, keeping to their various sides of the sidewalk, sensible only of the throbbing in their chests and the din in their heads.

The Epilogue to A.

Taking advantage of an unexpected opportunity, A. went on a journey. She set out, unencumbered and unreflecting as ever, after putting on her jeans, hanging the Nikon around her neck and throwing a few essentials into her knapsack (among other things, that selfsame comb and the purse decorated with beads were still there, but the apple was long gone; it had found its way, bitten but unfinished, into a garbage can, later disappearing without trace among the dizzying valleys of refuse dumps, and it is utterly implausible that even one of its six seeds should have germinated). In half a year she went through a good half of Europe with that knapsack, taking photographs, making friends, looking at things new and unknown. Finally she stopped in Prague, determined at whatever cost to become a pupil of Jan Saudek,[82] whom for some reason she considered her master. Naturally, she had to start by modeling for him in the nude. She posed in his shabby old studio, where even in summer the temperature never rose above 18 degrees, and the damp—the famous damp that gnaws away at the walls in his photographs—made her shiver, and the proliferation of mold brought on allergic reactions. But gradually—for that old fart Saudek could not fail to notice at least some tiny part of what Wozzeck had so loved and cherished—A. won his trust by her hard work, determination, pursuit of perfection (her circus training!) and ability to notice nuances and assimilate experience. Soon she had a new studio at her disposal, and it was no longer she who struck the deviant poses that Saudek invented. Instead, those who now spread themselves against the background of those same streaks and stains (embodiments of decay, but artificial this time) were young muscular pederasts and models with bright and whorish futures. A. really learned a great deal—not only to arrange light, to understand chemicals and the possibilities of optics, but to know what circumstances, conditions and moods here, in this world of three coordinates, would create the effect that she needed there, in the universe of flat vanities.

There were also
recurrals of curs
and recurrences of returns.

Later, when she entered the world of the Prague artistic underground, A. made a series of photographic portraits of its most striking representatives. Saudek helped her publish these as a separate album, and the album attracted attention. For an unknown emigrant this was success. Her first commissions, her first honoraria, covers of important magazines, conferences, receptions, castles in the air. Suddenly she had a studio of her own, her own models, she herself designed clothing for them, and some found this clothing interesting. There was a proposal for her own fashion label. Brilliant prospects seemed to open spontaneously. It turned out that during the smoky late-night hours that she spent in Prague rock dives A. had made a serious collection of audio recordings. It included aphorisms by various freethinkers, improvisations, unrepeatable in their undergroundness, by various musicians, shrieks from the brink by professional suicides, hyperpoetic effusions of morphine users, in short, it was going to be a veritable anthology of counterculture.

Yet at the pinnacle of her glory A. drops everything and returns home. Not alone, to be sure. Her companion is one of the Prague gurus, and he has been a guru for generations, for his father in his time had already been a leader of the renowned "Velvet Mothers of the Universe,"[83] and he, too, had suffered for being a guru (though evil tongues put it about that after 1968 he handed a lot of his friends over to the regime; still, where we know nothing, let us say nothing; in any case, he cut off his earthly path with his own hand and a dirty syringe and that divine liquor of the heroes of the underground, heroin). The son, too, was renowned as a nonconformist. After the second velvet revolution[84] he became a leader of the youth movement, participated in the loudest demonstrations by peace activists, Greenpeace supporters, new beatniks, etc. For a time he published the famous periodical *Revolt-Revue*,[85] and later still settled down, notwithstanding his tender years, as a bigwig at Radio Liberty after it moved to Prague from Munich.[86]

The immediate occasion of his trip with A. was the fact that his fiancée, a certain Aline Maurois (nothing about her is of interest to our story except her name),[87] was studying in Kyiv at the International School of Ukrainian Studies.[88] But he did not get to Kyiv, or rather, not right away, for when he visited A. at her home he tarried first a day, then two, and finally a month. Such was the approximate chronology. And yet things did not work out between them—perhaps the possibility of choosing tormented him, or perhaps his inborn and inbred sense of decorum prevented him from forgetting his fiancée so easily. In the end he left for Kyiv, promising to return soon. He kept his word insofar as he took a flight in the reverse direction, but, as frequently happens in cases of ballistic miscalculations, he landed some distance away—in the aforementioned ancient city of Prague. Apparently he sent A. letters containing explanations and propositions, but A., the wiser for her experiences (what wisdom, in point of fact, had her experiences taught her? none at all), set off on another journey. This time she was swept along a path taken in the previous century by sidelocked pilgrims from Galicia. This path led to Israel. But it was not Jerusalem that was the endpoint of her excursion. She stopped in a little town in the very south of the country. It had the promising name of Mejlakh-ha-Mavet[89] and had sprung up where there had been a kibbutz for repatriates from the lands around Warsaw. Among the unpretentious institutions of the place was an old people's home—part sanatorium, part asylum for the mentally incompetent. There A. unexpectedly found a job. Transplanted in their declining years into new soil, these East European goyim[90] naturally knew neither Sanskrit nor Swahili, let alone Yiddish or Hebrew. Old age took away their capacity to cope with their surroundings, accept new ways or understand why the promised land was so unlike Buchach, Vitsebsk or Przemyśl.[91] A spirit of profound autism ruled the sanatorium. Someone was needed to talk to the patients, wheelchair travelers to the end of their lives, in their native languages, usually Russian or Polish. The familiar sounds awakened echoes in hearts enervated by tedium, consciousness flickered in the depths of extinguished eyes, and collapsed lips twitched and twitched, how nice that you've come back, darling, how nice you've come back, do you remember?

Restoring these fragments of human souls was important to A. A whole world opened up before her—its history, the pale of settlement, expulsions, wars, the death of a favorite canary, the ghetto, Weinstock's pharmacy[92] at the corner of Kotsarska and Novolukashivska Streets, why, the child simply has to learn violin, gefilte fish, the enkayveedeegestapo,[93] Sophie dearest, you mustn't marry him, five-year plans, the nationality rubric in the passport,[94] he was most certainly well connected and drew quite a salary, and yet, packing cases and bags, mama, what do you need all that junk for, irritation, giving away the remainder of the wardrobe, selling the garage and the car, getting visas and.

Meanwhile ceaseless telephone calls came from Prague. A.'s mother decided that their quantity had turned into quality[95] and took the step of disclosing her daughter's telephone number in Israel, and for the first time in all the centuries since the exodus from Egypt a voice from Prague spoke through the receiver of a Mejlakh-ha-Mavet telephone. But soon after the first came a second, and a third, and soon this Czech-Jewish telephone link deserted the class of unique phenomena for the category of the mundane. These conversations were not cheap, and the descendant of the "Velvet Mothers" was obliged to sell his father's guitar—a rarity for which any collector would have paid a packet.

Well, that's more or less how it was.

And what of Wozzeck, some might ask. But who, frankly, would be interested in *that* moron with his lying about on his sofa and his drinking and his feelings? Let him lie.

Even so: what of Wozzeck?

A Story

So they tell him to get married. But he says no.

So he stays a bachelor for a bit, and then they talk him into courting a very rich and beautiful girl. On the wedding day they tie him up and cart him off to church. On the way back they see an old woman. He jumps onto a horse, and off he goes. That woman was none other than Thursday. So he gallops and gallops and gets to Friday. She says, "Don't worry. Everything's fine. Your death isn't expected anytime soon."

And she gives him an apple.

On he rides. He gets to Saturday, and Saturday says, "Your death isn't coming yet. Don't be afraid."

She gives him an apple, too.

He rides on and gets to Sunday. She also tells him not to be afraid. Then she gives him an apple and a scarf. As he leaves, Sunday says to him,

"If your death starts catching up with you, and you come to the sea, wave the scarf across it, and the sea will part. Cross to the other side, wave the other way, and the sea will join up again."

He gets to the sea, lets his horse graze and lies down to sleep, because he's very tired.

And then the old woman catches up with him. She tears the horse to pieces but doesn't dare touch him because those apples turn into great dogs and protect him.

He wakes up and sees the old woman, the serpent-woman. Then he remembers the scarf. He waves it, and the waters part. He walks to the other shore. There he meets a girl and begins to live with her.

Both Boyle and Mariotte[96]

The passage of years for That One had long ago become the passage of summers. He lived from summer to summer. Springs, winters, autumns passed, graceless, joyless, traceless, and only summer left a few marks in memory, like notches in a piece of wood.

He dedicated years to his struggle with A. It was hard work, like fighting a hydra. A.'s vitality was unbelievable. In one of the seasons he succeeded, by dint of intensive lying on the couch and drinking almond vodka, in reducing **A.** to the dimensions of **A.**, and over another especially auspicious (because rainy) summer, to **A.** But over autumn-winter-spring the calamitous A. grew back, exceeding even its previous dimensions. Then he tried vivisection. He dissected, he cut away, he shredded. Like a true scientist, he even tabulated his results:

22 June....................................... A.;
1 July... \.;
17 July..Λ.;
16 August................................. Δ.;
17 August..................................ʌ.;
1 September............................. ¯.;

but while he labored away on one side, the hydra A. invariably grew back on the other, until one summer he abandoned his vain attempts, realizing all of a sudden that he had lived with this for a long time, and nothing had happened to him, and nothing had happened at all, and the earth was not dying, nor disappearing, nor collapsing in shame at its own imperfection, and night followed day as before, and the sun had not begun to rise in the west, and the third part of the rivers was not made bitter, and so it was probably time to stop playing the martyr and inventing stories (not one of which you can finish, cowardly demiurge). It was time simply to live as other vegetables live—the pitchweed, the hedgewort, the fret-me-not, the philotendril, the protuberose, the succubent.[97]

That last summer he proved strangely prone to allergies. Probably because of the poplar fluff. It hung in the air, gathered in balls along paths and accumulated against skirting boards. Grass grew through it as if through snow. There could be no thought of opening a window or vent, for the room would fill at once with whole clots of this pale repellent matter. You constantly felt its irritating anemic touches on your face, and your vision could scarcely penetrate its dense mist.

That summer That One first experienced the so-called blind spots. He had read earlier that the human eye does not apprehend an image with the whole surface of the retina. The part where the optic nerve attaches itself to the orb of the eye is blind—it has no light-sensitive elements or photoreceptive cells.

He had also read about those diverting experiments by which you can demonstrate the existence of such a blind spot and with which the renowned Mariotte (*whom capricious and refractory destiny had wedded to the no less renowned Boyle, and thus they entered the history of physics and school textbooks as a Siamese monster by the name of Boyle-Mariotte*) entertained King Louis XIV, though he himself never managed to observe the disappearance of the royal head.

But it was not until that summer, against the white background of the poplar mist, that he noticed indistinct black spots constantly accompanying his gaze wherever he looked. Now every representation—faces, landscapes, pages and walls, bodies and advertisements, and sky and water and absolutely, absolutely everything had this minor flaw, this defect: two tiny spots. This tempted him to become demanding and fastidious: when selecting, say, a shirt in a shop or sitting down at a table in a cafe or lying down on a hotel bed, to demand that the housemaid, salesperson or waiter make endless changes and exchanges, heeding no apologies, explanations or denials; and stubbornly to insist on his point (everyone shared the same structure of the eye, and so they should see the same thing!), to complain, pick and choose, fall into hysterics, make scandals, throw articles of clothing around the room, tear tablecloths from tables and sheets from beds; and finally to get the reputation of a whinger and a malcontent and become the terror of every establishment and...and what? The temptations remained temptations only. After all, he never went to cafes or spent nights at hotels, and it was years since he had bought a new shirt. And, in any case, to whom could he complain, for example, about blemishes on a cloudy sky, a fresh covering of snow or that selfsame poplar fluff? So he had to get used to this inconvenience as well. He had to get used to many things, for example:

—that the topography of his face was changing irreversibly. New furrows and gullies appeared and deepened day by day, so that even the famous Gillette Slalom Plus could not negotiate them, and so there was no need to spend money on this plaything;

—that the skin beneath his eyes was taking on more and more the color of parchment, while on his nose the capillaries turned shamelessly purple, betraying passions that in any case were not so very secret;

—that it was becoming ever harder to battle deposits of fat, flaccidity of muscles, stiffness of joints and morning swellings;

—that the color of his tongue indicated chronically neglected ailments, plans for the treatment of which were becoming increasingly anachronistic;

—that the terrors of the night were becoming invincible;

—that the stars in the heavens were only one of the productions in God's theater;[98]

—that the absence of will and desire had to be compensated by inertia;

—that there is no atonement for your greatest sin, despair;

—that alcohol had long ago begun to take more than it gave;

—that the hair on your body, which (both hair and body) had once so excited her, was becoming long, curly and repulsive, and hair is generally a problem, for if it disappears from your head, then for some reason it appears in great clumps in your nostrils (miserable exchange!), and it also turns gray in the most unexpected places, and it is hair into which that precious down on the skin is transformed—that down which, according to Notnabokov's definition, "swaddles the fruit of trees of the almond group," and which (down, that is) should not be confused with the poplar fluff that turned this summer into a paranoia of allergies, as a result of which That One finally became aware of blind spots in front of his eyes—how much he had failed to see in the course of his life because of them!—blind moldy spots, dramatically demonstrated by the genius Mariotte, now inseparably fused with Boyle—his was a bitter, tragic life, and yet certainly less tragic than that of Gay-Lussac,[99] whom the schoolboys of my childhood dissected into two cripples—Gay and Lussac, and whom the cynical schoolchildren of today simply sneer at as the gay Lussac, although...who knows? who knows? Perhaps they are right after all.

Enemies and Collaborators

I don't have so many enemies. At least, you can count them on the fingers of your hands. If you have so many fingers and so many hands. They number exactly 26. Let us recall them by name: A., B., C., D., E., F., G., H., I., J., K., L., M., N., O., P., Q., R., S., T., U., V., W., X., Y., Z. Or like this: "a.," "b.," "c.," "d.," "e.," "f.," "g.," "h.," "i.," "j.," "k.," "l.," "m.," "n.," "o.," "p.," "q.," "r.," "s.," "t.," "u.," "v.," "w.," "x.," "y.," "z." Even individually they constitute a terrible force. And together they are simply invincible. Or like this: "I., N., V., I., N., C., I., B., L., E." Or, finally, like this: "i.," "n.," "v.," "i.," "n.," "c.," "i.," "b.," "l.," "e."

But perhaps I'm wrong. Perhaps a cat is no more than a warm itinerant continent for fleas. And a loaf of bread is but the embodiment of an architectonic ideal for urbanized Egyptian ants. And my beloved is just a collection of microflora.

During the long years of the liberation struggle I honed to the point of virtuosity my skill in identifying among many telephone numbers the numbers of collaborators. The secret police always gives its recruits numbers that are easy to remember with the help of a specially devised system of mnemonics. Take, for example, 6 23 71 8. Here we see a six that is confirmed by the following product of the two and the three (6=2x3), as well as by the difference between the seven and the one (7-1=6). Those same seven and one, summed together, are the key for remembering the eight (7+1=8). But the secret is not always so simple and obvious. Usually the code is put together in such a way that the uninitiated eye notices nothing. Sometimes apparent simplicity conceals only the first key, and after that you have to crack an appalling number of additional ones. The more complex the mnemonic system, the more important the agent's place in the hierarchy of collaborators. The highest levels of initiation—and this usually means working for several masters, maneuvering between warring groups, and direct access to the levers of power—are rewarded with codes that cannot be broken by simple arithmetic means. Such numbers call for a knowledge of higher mathematics—logarithms, differentials, theory of numbers. And inasmuch as almost everyone is a collaborator, it is only the fact that the broad masses do not know this higher mathematics that prevents us from discovering in our home telephone number a confirmation of our membership of the elect.

P.S.: Should you come across a strangely simple or suspiciously symmetrical number (1,000,001, for example, or 666999), be aware that you are dealing not with a collaborator but with a primitive and legitimate general of counterintelligence or the security service.

Sheol

That summer he suddenly had the idea of writing a book. It happened when he became aware of himself as a character in somebody's text—even if it was his own. This awareness would excuse him from abiding by generally accepted laws and rules, attending to structure, plot or vocabulary, worrying about the reader or thinking about the unity of the work. After all, authors usually present works created by their characters in a fragmentary way, sometimes contenting themselves with a few brushstrokes. Most often, instead of having the character really write something, the author simply presents a summary of his own ideas, assigning to the character all possible and impossible copyrights.

And so he, That-One-unto-himself, author-unto-himself, character-unto-himself, had the idea of constructing (or merely reporting on) a text that would be as hermetic and self-enclosed as it was symmetrical and suicidal. In fact, there would be two texts, or two parts of the one, and they would contradict each other. Each part might assert, mean or narrate something, but that "something" would invariably be ruined and destroyed by the other. Khomsky[100] would probably call these parts mutually apophatic (and probably he would do so ironically). The great blind Jorge[101] would doubtless speak of two mirrors gazing into the endless row of their mutual reflections. Liubansky would bring in light and darkness, body and soul, grog and bog, bread and wine, guilt and atonement, the "yes" and the "no," Yin and Yang, the shadow and the day, the night and the sword and much else besides, blossom and decay, honey and wormwood, space and time, yours and mine, towers and powers, gods and sods, sleep and forgetting, being and nonbeing, hell and heaven, raves and drives, highs and dives, the great in the small, the silence and the song, mercy and anger, sea and land, the wet and the dry, eros and death, and this and that, laughter and tears, sacredness and sin, feasts and fasts, the loose and the tight, jazz and rock. That is why Liubansky is a prophet.

But That One had not read anything for a long time, he knew neither Khomsky nor Liubansky, and he had long forgotten Borges. He did not even guess at the existence of a witty novel by the good-looking Solange Mariott (Solange Miriam) titled *Rien du tout, ou la conséquence,*[102] which embodied an almost similar idea.

Almost, but not quite.

That One found ways of annihilating literally all aspects of the text, of forcing the beautiful up against the ugly, of transforming the sublime into the ridiculous, of disguising tragedy as farce. But neither tragedy nor farce would be conclusive. They would disappear as soon as they touched each other, as electric charges disappear when positive touches negative. That One worked out how to make his plots plotless and cast into doubt any action, statement or fact. Nothing would be known with certainty. He knew how to make his characters intangible—none would have the right to be constant, defined or lifelike; from time to time each would disintegrate into several, or metamorphose into someone else. Even the protagonist would disappear in the end into the jungle of his own self-indulgent gibberish.

But even this was not enough for the ambitious debutant. That One resolved by means of similar punitive manipulations to eliminate first the author, whose shadowy idol looms behind every page of every book, and then to annihilate language itself. He knew that the only tool available for its destruction would be that selfsame language, but he was not intimidated. On the contrary, he took great pleasure in imagining how language, that abhorrent monster, having devoured all, would begin to devour itself, turning itself inside out like a glove, unwillingly regurgitating the prisoners it had just swallowed, and would start again at the beginning, only to destroy everything once more in its efforts finally to get at itself. That One, who knew that no victory was possible in this war, thought this would be the greatest revenge of which the human being is capable.

That One wanted to avoid a tediously linear or even unilinear text and the necessity of reading from the beginning to the end or at least of being aware of a beginning and an end. Similar tasks had preoccupied the above-mentioned Cortázar without success. Neither of the mirrors that face each other is allowed to be the first. It is impossible to differentiate between the mirror itself and its reflection in another mirror. You can only gaze into empty space, guessing at another behind it, and behind that one yet another, and another.

Furthermore, those who enter this world, this book, will never find a way out and will wander amidst nonexistent things, among myriad copies of their own "I" that burn in the fire of incessant annihilation.

But plans remain plans until the first word is written. The question is, which word is the first in a book that has no beginning?

That One bought an enormously fat notebook and an unbreakable Koh-i-Noor pencil, and one July night, sitting in the kitchen in a cloud of tobacco smoke, he slowly and painstakingly wrote: *The Return...* And suddenly the perfection of his own design became a drawback. He realized that he had to write both parts simultaneously, otherwise a hierarchy based on primacy would inevitably emerge. It always makes itself felt. You can't fool or avoid it. And although the difference in the first phrases might be quite inconsequential ("The Return of Pain" or "Coming Down"—what difference did that make, one might ask), yet That One felt that he would be unable to cross the petty barrier thrown up by any further letter, any mark, any full stop. For that would mean leaping over oneself, over the perfection of the idea, that would mean creating an untruth.

Departure of the Heroes

Well, that would seem to be all. Everyone has been found a place. I've slotted everybody in somewhere or other. Wozzeck is locked up in a room that has recently been painted white (today he has no pain: I mercifully grant him a day's respite), That One keeps on *returning*, that dear little graphomaniac of ours, That One, and I am sitting at my desk, saying good-bye to the heroes of "Night" and "Day."

There goes Miriam. First one, then another, a third, a hundredth. Farewell, Miriam. Forgive me, but I never loved you at all.

There goes Pepa, the genius and illegal immigrant to Canada, a part of my "I" that I am unlikely ever to meet again.

There goes Marta, regal and godlike Marta, doomed, doomed soul that she is.

There goes the Cyclops, my best schoolmate, honorary citizen of the land of dreams.

There goes Gorwitz, or more precisely, there he doesn't go, because he's got drunk somewhere again, that damned alkie, and now it's not so easy to get rid of him.

There goes Karp, the unsurpassable Liubansky, to whom I owe almost everything and without whom this story almost certainly would not exist.

There go Nestor, Putsyk, Nigel, Yukhan, Caesar and Gantenbein.

There go the Borovchaks, the Gustavs, the Sacher-Masochs, the Schulzes, the Maupassants and the Schwarzkopfs in serried ranks, and after them, sporting a child's tin drum and short pants, Adenauer-père.

There goes Siana, the girl who taught me the shortest word beginning with "p."

There goes Sasha-Abrasha, whom I undeservedly offended. Thanks for those *Playboys*, Sashko.

There goes Iris Murdoch, author of the excellent novel *Bruno's Dream*, Nigel's mum.

There goes Aline Maurois, uninteresting except for her name.

There goes the literary fraternity—Kamidian, Borakne, Irpinets, Andrusiak, Bryhynets, Malkovych, Izdryk, Zabuzhko, Lysheha, Rymaruk, Herasymiuk, Luhosad, the Tsyperdiuks (Ivan and Dima), Protsiuk, combatant Dovhy, Fishbein, Lybon, Avzhezh and Pozaiak. And where is Hrytsenko?

There goes the equilibrist Mokhói. They say he has perfected his number and now balances on a pole while supporting in his hands a whole pyramid of plates, cups, saucepans and crystal goblets. Apart from that, he ordered himself a magnificent body stocking bristling with synthetic thorns and now at last looks just like a young medieval devil.

There goes Kudusai. He goes, leaving me only A.'s portrait—there it is in front of me on the wall—a strange, troubling portrait, scarcely like her at all. The capricious Matiash has changed even the color of her eyes and hair, and yet it is she, undoubtedly it is she, my beloved, this profile, this all-seeing gaze, this half-open mouth—the embodiment of my dream and of her.

There they all go, even those whom I have not named, whom I have forgotten, whom I have ignored, and only A. does not go.

Not ever.

From time to time news of her reaches you. At first this caused you acute pain (it was especially distressing to find in the journal *Fotografie* a photo by Saudek where she is nude and kissing a man's hand—how many impure, lustful, lascivious or simply indifferent eyes are able without the merest hindrance to look upon her body, the body that belongs only to you!), but now—now it's not too bad, you've reconciled yourself to it. Well, whether you like it or not, from time to time news of her reaches you: now she has returned from Israel, now she has gone to the States with her Prague fiancé, there her path briefly disappears, but soon she appears on television with Versace—cordial embraces, partnership, the society pages, a trip together to Florida, gossip; then a series of shattering press reports from Bosnia, her voice coming from the very inferno of military action. Then another quiet break, then rumors, probably invented, of a marriage with a national hero who is also a colonel in the Serbian army, then London, a festival of computer-generated art—she was a success at this, too—and so on without end, year in, year out, there was no end to the global carousel of your sufferings, it was as if time were not moving, as if life were simply a series of experiments, as if there were no danger of aging or death, as if A. were not A. but Ahasuerus. Why, here it is at last, the promised secret of the name, the last but least falsehood, lie or untruth of the day. It is evening, and the time has come to say farewell, Alcestis, antigone, Ariadne, asthenia, Anna Perenna, apathy, Annabelle, alice, Aurelia, aberration, Alaska my dear, antoinette, Analogy, astrology, Anemia, dearest allergy, Neborak's Amalia, andromache, Autonomy, assyria, Algebra, anastasia, Anesthesia, atrophy, Amazon, atmosphere, O Alphabet mine. Till the morrow.

"Till the morrow," you pronounce in a low voice, leaving of the "I-you-he" only a trace of the nonexistent "I." Exhausted and miserable, you fall asleep, and as you sink into the warm waves of somnolence you weakly mutter some belated *prayers,*

imploring that the day die down quickly, that this long and lonely "Day" should pass, float by and perish and that, God willing, you yourself should end, and only your soul have neither end nor limit (not ever, in no place and not for anything, in no way and not in the least degree), but only peace and forgetting.

"Our Father, Which art in Heaven, hallowed be Thy Name, Thy Kingdom come, Thy will be done on earth as it is in Heaven. Give us this day our daily bread, and forgive us our trespasses as we forgive them that trespass against us. And lead us not into temptation, but deliver us from evil. For Thine is the Kingdom, the power and the glory, now and forever. Amen.
Lord Jesus Christ, have mercy on me
Lord Jesus Christ, have mercy on me
Lord Jesus Christ, have mercy on me
Lord Jesus Christ,
have mercy on me
Lord
Jesus Christ,
have mercy on me
Lord
Jesus
Christ, have mer
cy on
m e
Lo
rd Je sus
Chri
s t, h a
ve me
r
c
y
o n m e

NOTES

Annotating Izdryk's works has a certain tradition. The publication of *Wozzeck* in 1997 was followed the next year by the appearance of a densely printed 28–page brochure titled *Wozzeckurgy Bet: A Commentary on the "Inner Encyclopedia" of Izdryk's Novel* Wozzeck (Volodymyr Ieshkiliev, *Votstsekurhiia Bet: Komentari do "vnutrishn'oï entsyklopediï" romanu Izdryka "Votstsek"* [Ivano-Frankivsk: Unikornus, 1998]). *The Island of Krk* contained thirty-eight pages of annotations by Izdryk himself, and *Double Leon* came with an entire critical apparatus: Leonid Kosovych's "Postscript," a series of essays on the more recondite aspects of the text, a glossary of foreign words, and the annotations themselves. These annotations offer far more than the customary explanations and contextualizations. They are extensions of the aesthetic structure of Izdryk's main texts, securing for readers the pleasure of privileged knowledge or engaging them in games of mystification. They serve as testimonies to the profoundly intertextual quality of Izdryk's works and as signposts of his emphatic participation in what Yuri Andrukhovych referred to on the back cover of *Wozzeck* as "all that (pardon the expression) postmodernism."

Izdryk himself professed to harbor a characteristically ambiguous attitude toward annotations. He piously asserted that "regardless of whether the reader knows particular facts, or grasps hidden allusions or explicit quotations, good literature should speak for itself and do its own work." On the other hand, he confessed that "as a reader I desperately love annotations and always immerse myself in them with delight.... It is precisely because they are so catastrophically bereft of annotations that I never buy popular novels. Oh, how those worn-out plots and dull images would sparkle, how sonorously the most banal phrases would resound, if a real master took in hand the business of the commentary! As Borges said, 'the beautiful is widely distributed and lies in wait for us on random pages of a mediocre author, or in dialogues heard on the street'" (Izdryk, "Avtokomentar," in *Ostriv Krk ta inshi istoriï* [Ivano-Frankivsk: Lileia-NV, 1998], 77–117, here 79).

Yeshkiliev's annotations to *Wozzeck* are themselves as much a *tour de force* as the novel itself. The generous material that they encompass is of several kinds. Allusions to little-known persons, places and facts are explained. Many, though by no means all, quotations, explicit and hidden, exact and approximate, are sourced. These philological niceties received Izdryk's mock approval: "The majority of [Yeshkiliev's] annotations are correct, interesting and informative. After all, as a person of academic tradition and discipline he checked them with me whenever uncertainties arose" ("Iurii Izdryk: Rozmovy pro literaturu, 'Chetver,' muzyku etc." [Interview with Kateryna Hichan], *e-motion knyhy*, 27 September–3 October 2005, no. 29 <http://www.e-motion.com.ua/issue29/books/roof/Jur_j_zdrik1.html>, accessed 18 April 2006). This, of course, is a parodic understatement of what Yeshkiliev is about. *Wozzeckurgy Bet* has (or affects) the ambition of shaping the reader's encounter with the novel—in a sense, of *creating* Izdryk's novel anew and in full. The very title, modeled as it is on the words "demiurgy" and "alphabet," implies this. As the demiurge in Plato was the maker of the material world, so Yeshkiliev would create *Wozzeck* in the image of his aesthetic theory, which proposes that the activity of the artist produces worlds enclosed in themselves, subject to their own rules, and alternative to the world so uncertainly attested by common experience. *Wozzeckurgy Bet* is replete with long interpretive excursuses, always ironic and self-ironic, couched in the jargon of literary theory. Izdryk's text emerges from just the first two pages of *Wozzeckurgy Bet* as the carrier of "demiurgic signs," "deconstructive irony," "narrative space" (5), the "encyclopedic debility syndrome," "informational and hermeneutic paradoxes," "epistemological discourse" (6), and much else.

The following annotations set themselves a more modest task. They aim to explain references to names, places and facts unlikely to be familiar; to decode for the English-speaking reader allusions to Ukrainian realia, both Soviet and post-Soviet; where possible, to specify the sources of direct quotations; and, finally, to clarify allusions where they are important for grasping some aspect of the thought or form of the text. Of course, these annotations cannot but owe a profound debt to Yeshkiliev's erudition and local knowledge, and this is acknowledged repeatedly below. Occasionally it makes sense simply to quote Yeshkiliev. In such cases, where additional detail is needed, it is added in brackets.

[1] *Palimpsest.* A manuscript erased to accommodate fresh text, but with the original text still readable.

[2] *O child, O sister mine, let's hence to lands where you and I shall never parted be.* The first lines of Charles Baudelaire's poem "L'invitation au voyage" (Invitation to the Voyage) from *Les Fleurs du mal* (The Flowers of Evil, 1857). Yeshkiliev (5) speculates that the quotation is mediated through the Russian translation that Izdryk may have known from David Tukhmanov's compact disc *Po volne moiei pamiati* (On the Wave of my Memory), which includes a setting of the poem in Irina Ozerova's translation.

[3] *Why the Apostle of Truth and Knowledge fails to come.* A quotation from a quatrain composed in 1860 by Ukraine's most celebrated poet, Taras Shevchenko (1814–1861): "I den' ide, i nich ide. / I, holovu skhopyvshy v ruky, / Dyvuieshshia, chomu ne ide / Apostol pravdy i nauky" (The day goes by, the night goes by. / And, your head clasped in your hands, / You wonder why / the apostle of truth and knowledge does not come).

[4] For an account of the prehistory of the name "Wozzeck," see the Introduction.

[5] *Wilson chambers, electron guns, Doppler accelerators and Foucault's pendulums.* The Scottish physicist Charles Thomas Rees Wilson (1869–1959) invented the Wilson cloud chamber, a device used for the study of the behavior of charged nuclear particles, in 1912. Electron guns, most familiar through their use in television tubes, are devices that produce and direct streams of electrons. The Austrian physicist Christian Doppler (1803–1853) showed that the properties of light and sound waves vary, depending upon the relative motion of the source and the observer. His name is not connected with particle accelerators (instruments used for research into the atomic and subatomic structure of matter). Jean-Bernard-Léon Foucault (1819–1868) used a freely suspended pendulum in 1851 to demonstrate the rotation of the earth about its axis. The Foucault pendulum has no connection to the study of the component particles of matter. The allusion here may rather be to the novel *Pendolo di Foucault* (Foucault's Pendulum, 1988) by Umberto Eco (b. 1932), widely recognized as representative of the postmodern approach to writing that Izdryk's *Wozzeck* also exemplifies.

[6] *Coulomb's law.* The French physicist Charles-Augustin de Coulomb (1736–1806) formulated a law that expressed the force between charged particles as dependent on the strength of the charges and the distance between them.

[7] *Sacher-Masoch.* The German-language novelist Leopold von Sacher-Masoch (1836–1895) is best known for his novel *Venus im Pelz* (Venus in Furs, 1870) and its treatment of the theme of sexual satisfaction derived from subjugation and pain. In 1886 the Viennese psychologist Richard von Krafft-Ebing named the corresponding sexual inclination "masochism." Sacher-Masoch was born in Lviv and spent the first twelve years of his life there. According to some accounts, he returned in 1860 to lecture on history at Lviv University. Several of his works, including the novel *Don Juan von Kolomea* (Don Juan from Kolomyia, 1872) and *Galizische Geschichten* (Galician Stories, 1876), are set in western Ukraine.

[8] *Schulz.* The Jewish writer and artist Bruno Schulz (1892–1942), who made a major contribution to Polish modernist prose, was born in the western Ukrainian city of Drohobych, where he spent most of his life and where, during the German occupation, he was murdered by the Gestapo. Interest in his work in Ukraine grew during the 1990s and especially after 2001, when murals that he had painted were discovered in a building in Drohobych. These were removed in circumstances never fully explained, reappearing shortly afterwards in Jerusalem.

[9] *Stryi.* A small city about sixty kilometers south of Lviv.

[10] *Pepa.* A character of this name appears in other works by Izdryk, including *The Island of Krk,* which contains the following annotation: "I have written so much about Pepa, my colleague from the Institute, that there is no point in repeating any of it here. I do not think that there is a single work of mine in which he does not appear in one way or another" (*Ostriv Krk* [Ivano-Frankivsk: Lileia-NV, 1998], 90). The note reproduces, "almost in full," a two-page story attributed to Pepa (91–92). Texts authored by Pepa appeared in *Chetver* and on the *Proza* web page. In his long conversation with Taras Prokhasko published in the *Inshyi format* series, Izdryk referred to "the legendary Anton Seliukh and Pepa" as coinitiators of *Chetver* (Taras Prokhasko, *Izdryk* [Ivano-Frankivsk: Lileia-NV, 2003], 40). A character called

Artur Pepa appears in Yuri Andrukhovych's novel *Dvanadtsiat' obruchiv* (Twelve Rings, 2003). Yeshkiliev (8) surmises that Pepa corresponds to Pavlo Turko, one of the founding coeditors of *Chetver.*

[11] *Goldberg Variations on a theme from a Chinese Chang rondo.* Johann Sebastian Bach's "Goldberg" variations (BWV 988, 1742) are the most notable of his compositions for harpsichord. The rondo is a musical form characterized by alternation between a repeated theme and new themes. "Chang" is a Chinese character and a word meaning "to sing." In response to this annotator's query about the meaning of "Chinese Chang rondo," Izdryk replied: "The 'rondo,' as is well known, is a cyclical musical form. 'Chang' is an imitation of a Chinese nominal lexeme. Taken together, 'Chinese Chang rondo' is a construction bereft of content or connotation and may therefore be translated arbitrarily."

[12] *Dwarf director who somehow resembled Sebastian Moro.* See the painting by Diego Velázquez (1599–1660) "El nan Sebastian de Morra" (The Dwarf Sebastian de Morra, 1645).

[13] *Cicadas on the Cyclades.* "Cykady na Cykladach" (Cicadas on the Cyclades) is a song by the Polish rock band Maanam, founded in 1976.

[14] *People are OK, God bless them. As for things—you can put up with them, too. But plants and animals are sometimes intolerable.* A joke at the expense of the German philosopher Martin Heidegger (1889–1976). An issue of Izdryk's journal *Chetver*, structured as a series of parodic encyclopedia entries, contained an entry titled "Heidegger." This was not an expository text about the philosopher but a translation of a sizable excerpt from Heidegger's lecture of 1946, "Wozu Dichter?" ("Haidehher [Heidegger] Martin," *Chetver*, 1992, no. 1 [3]: 41–45, including "Nashcho poet?" [What Are Poets For?], translated by Iurii Prokhas'ko). In his lecture Heidegger analyzed minutely one of the late poems of Rainer Maria Rilke, especially those of its lines that refer to the ways in which human beings, on the one hand, and plants and animals, on the other, are "wagered" by Nature and for their part acquiesce in this wager (*Wagnis*) through an act of their will. Heidegger's discussion is long, subtle and painstaking (see Martin Heidegger, *Gesamtausgabe*, vol. 5 [Frankfurt am Main: Vittorio Klostermann,

1977], 269–320). Izdryk's two-line quip about people, things, plants and animals, by contrast, is brief, brutal and irreverent.

[15] *Pagan girls love sex in the long grass, especially in summer.* "A paraphrase of Poem IV of Andrukhovych's cycle 'Letters to Ukraine': Ukrainian girls are musical. They love / having sex in the grass, especially in summer" (Yeshkiliev, 11). Andrukhovych's "Lysty v Ukraïnu" appeared in *Chetver*, 1993, no. 4: 55–62.

[16] *Ypres.* The German army used a poison gas—chlorine—in battle for the first time at Ypres in 1915. Mustard gas (dichlorethylsulphide), known in French as *yperite*, was first used at Ypres somewhat later, in 1917.

[17] *Guy de Maupassant's* A Life. The French naturalist writer Maupassant (1850–1893), acclaimed for his short stories, was also the author of full-length novels, including *Une Vie* (A Life, 1883), in English translation often titled *A Woman's Life*. Yeshkiliev remarks that *A Life* was "one of the few books, alongside Leo Taxil's *Amusing Bible* and Boccaccio's *Decameron*, that served the chaste pupil of the Soviet era as a textbook on the sexual life" (12).

[18] *You dreamt not of Montpensier, not of a montagnard, not of Wes Montgomery on Montparnasse*. The shared syllable "mont" brings together, respectively, the Duchesse de Montpensier (1627–1693), a princess of the French royal house and an opponent of the crown in the wars of the Fronde; a radical deputy to the National Convention at the time of the French Revolution; the African-American jazz guitarist Wes Montgomery (1925–1968); and the section of Paris renowned in the first part of the twentieth century for its remarkable concentration of writers and artists, many of them from outside France.

[19] *Bel-Ami.* A novel by Maupassant published in 1885.

[20] *Roksolana.* Nastia Lisovska (1505–1561), born in Rohatyn in western Ukraine, was taken captive during a Tatar raid and brought to Constantinople, where she became a member of the Sultan's harem and, as the most powerful wife of Suleiman the Magnificent, exercised considerable influence over Ottoman politics. In Ukrainian literature the Roksolana motif has often served as a basis for imaginative treatments of the theme of national identity and its maintenance or loss in foreign

environments. Izdryk's focus on the erotic dimensions of the story was anticipated in a short book, *Zhytie haremnoie* (Life in the Harem, 1996), by a writer renowned for his black humor and sexual explicitness, Yuri Vynnychuk (b. 1952). Needless to say, there is no condition that medical science has classified as the "Roksolana complex."

[21] *Hotel California came much later. Hotel California,* the best-selling album of the American rock group "Eagles," was released in 1976.

[22] *As in Magritte.* See the painting "La philosophie dans le boudoir" (Philosophy in the Boudoir, 1948) by the Belgian surrealist artist René Magritte (1898–1967).

[23] *Ollie (Nigel).* As Yeshkiliev (13) points out, the hypothesis that the allusion here is to the character of Nigel in one of the works of the British novelist and philosopher Iris Murdoch (1919–1999) is borne out by a sentence that occurs in the chapter "Departure of the Heroes": "There goes Iris Murdoch, author of the excellent novel *Bruno's Dream,* Nigel's mum."

[24] *Karp Liubansky.* According to Yeshkiliev (13), a character in the trilogy *Miracles* by the Macedonian novelist Slavko Janevski (1920–2000). The figure of whom Karp Liubansky is a portrait is, most likely, Yuri Andrukhovych (b. 1960), the best known of the Ukrainian writers who achieved prominence in the late 1980s and early 1990s through the provocativeness of their works. Known as the "patriarch" of the avant-gardist triad "Bu-Ba-Bu," Andrukhovych commenced his literary career as a poet and author of short stories. His fame was secured by the scandal surrounding the publication of his novel *Rekreatsiï* (1992), translated into English by this commentator as *Recreations* and published by the Canadian Institute of Ukrainian Studies Press in 1998. His subsequent novels were *Moskoviiada* (The Moscoviad, 1993), *Perverziia* (1996), translated into English by Michael M. Naydan as *Perverzion* (2005), and *Dvanadtsiat' obruchiv* (Twelve Rings, 2003), translated into German by Sabine Stöhr as *Zwölf Ringe* (2005).

[25] *Joachim (Yukhan).* Yeshkiliev (14) speculates that this name is borrowed from that of the character Joachim Hencke in the novel *Homo Faber* (1957) by the Swiss writer and dramatist Max Frisch (1911–1991).

[26] *Matiash Kudusai.* "The slightly transformed name [from Matte Kudasai] of a composition in the album *Discipline* by the group 'King Crimson'" (Yeshkiliev, 14).

[27] *Gippius.* Izdryk replaces the name of a common aquarium fish, the guppy, with the surname of the Russian symbolist poet Zinaida Gippius (1869–1945).

[28] *Koh-i-Noor.* The name of a Czech art supplies firm. In the Soviet Union the imported Koh-i-Noor pencil enjoyed a reputation for high quality.

[29] *Adenauer, the only luminary who remained after Heidegger's ignominious flight.* Konrad Adenauer (1876–1967) was chancellor of the Federal Republic of Germany from 1949 to 1963, during the period of economic recovery following the Second World War. Martin Heidegger (1889–1976), the German philosopher whose philosophy of being and contribution to existentialist thought greatly impressed Izdryk and others associated with the Stanislav Phenomenon (see the Introduction), joined the Nazi party in 1933 and remained a member until the end of the war. This may be the "ignominious flight" to which the text refers. The apotheosis of Adenauer suggests that, following the defeat of the philosophical Europe represented by Heidegger's defection, an Adenauerian Europe attuned to pragmatism and economics has come to the fore. The heroes of Ukrainian alternative literature are not spared inclusion in this diminished Europe: they, too, are members of the "tribe of Adenauer."

[30] *Chateaubriand.* The reason for the inclusion of the French diplomat and Romantic writer François-René de Chateaubriand (1768–1848) in the genealogy is mysterious.

[31] *Cyclops.* According to Yeshkiliev, the name of the one-eyed giants in Greek mythology served as the nickname of one of Izdryk's school friends (15).

[32] *Godot.* In the absurdist play *Waiting for Godot* (1952) by the Irish playwright Samuel Beckett (1906–1989) the character of Godot, keenly awaited, never comes.

[33] *Marquet's boats.* The French painter Albert Marquet (1875–1947), a representative of Fauvism, often painted harbor scenes.

[34] *Galician colloquialism.* "Galicia" (Halychyna in Ukrainian) is the historical name of the westernmost Ukrainian ethnic lands. It was also the name of a medieval principality, and from 1772 to 1918 of a province of the Austrian Empire encompassing Ukrainian and Polish ethnic territories. Differences between the language spoken by the Ukrainians of Galicia and their compatriots in the central and eastern Ukrainian lands within the Russian Empire persisted well into the twentieth century. The nostalgia for Central Europe articulated by some writers of the Stanislav Phenomenon included nostalgia for Galician linguistic distinctiveness. The second part of the *Chetver* manifesto, signed by Izdryk, Pepa and Anton Seliukh and dated 1990 but published in 1999, is an apologia for the "Galician language." It commences as follows: "The world does not look so bad when, properly lit, it is reflected in a cup of decent coffee. The Galician language is that coffee, poured into the porcelain cup that is the geographical center of Europe" ("Chetverhovyi manifest," *Chetver*, 1999, no. 8: 15–18, here 16).

[35] *Iskanderian enthusiasts.* The writer Fazil Iskander (b. 1929) is probably mentioned in this context because his homeland is Abkhazia, a part of Georgia that is *de facto* autonomous and fought a war against Georgia in 1992–93.

[36] *Briukhovychi.* A suburb of Lviv northwest of the city.

[37] *The kind that have a taste for folkloric vests, trembitas and Easter eggs, who decorate their quarters with Hutsul kilims and the Taras-Ivan-Lesia triad.* The *trembita* is a woodwind instrument several meters long used in the Carpathian Mountains mainly for giving notice of a death. In most regions of Ukraine Easter eggs are intricately decorated by a process that involves repeated dyeing and the application of molten wax. The Hutsuls are the native inhabitants of parts of the Carpathian Mountains. They maintained their rich customs and crafts, including the weaving of kilims, well into the twentieth century, when these activities became objects of interest for tourists and symbols of ethnic authenticity. The poet Taras Shevchenko (1814–1861), the writer and intellectual Ivan Franko (1856–1916) and the poet and playwright Lesia Ukrainka (1871–1913) constitute the heart of the traditional Ukrainian literary canon.

[38] *Neither Kyiv nor Halych nor least of all Krylos, but Kolomyia.* Each of the first three places in this series has a claim to being the capital of a state on Ukrainian territory. In the Middle Ages, Halych was the capital of the Principality of Galicia-Volhynia. The actual location of the medieval city of Halych corresponds not to modern Halych but to the village of Krylos. Kolomyia, on the other hand, is the "capital" of Hutsul culture.

[39] *The glorious Dnipro, swollen somewhat by rumor, whose center can be reached only by the most audacious and hardiest of avians.* An allusion to a famous passage in praise of the Dnipro River by the Russian-language writer of Ukrainian parentage Nikolai Gogol (Mykola Hohol, 1809–1852) in his story "Strashnaia mest'" (The Terrible Judgment), included in his *Vechera na khutore bliz Dikanki* (Evenings on a Farm near Dikanka, 1831–32): "But they [the woods and wild flowers reflected in the Dnipro] dare not look into the Dnieper in midstream; none but the sun and the blue sky gaze into it there. Rarely will a bird fly as far as that. Glorious one! There is no river like it in the world" (quoted from Nikolai V. Gogol, *Tales of Good and Evil*, trans. David Magarshack [London: John Lehmann, 1949], 45).

[40] *Godforsaken Kyiv.* A number of authors associated with the Stanislav Phenomenon, including Yuri Andrukhovych, affected a deeply ambiguous attitude to Ukraine's capital, regarding it as well outside the cultural and geographical orbit of the Central Europe that they cherished.

[41] *That white-columned Arcadia, that Livadia.* Arcadia was a province of ancient Greece that became the symbol of unspoiled natural beauty and harmony. Livadia is a picturesque part of Yalta in the Crimea where a palace was built for the Russian tsar Nicholas II.

[42] *In the words of the entomological Grand Master, "swaddles the fruit of trees of the almond group."* Yeshkiliev detects here, without specifying the exact source, a quotation from the Russian émigré novelist Vladimir Nabokov (1899–1977), who wrote in Russian and English, and whose works are characterized by as high a level of artistic self-consciousness as Izdryk's. Nabokov was also a distinguished collector of butterflies and a master of chess. The passage is quoted from the autobiographical text *Drugie berega* (Other Shores) (New York: Izdatel'stvo imeni Chekhova, 1954), 98–99.

[43] *Some denizen of Cro-Magnon or other.* Skeletons found in the Cro-Magnon rock shelter at Les Eyzies in France in 1868 are among the earliest that belong to representatives of *homo sapiens* in Europe.

[44] *Holothurians, ascidians, ophiuroids.* Species of sea life also known by more common names: sea cucumbers, sea squirts, and brittle stars.

[45] *Buridan's ass.* The name of the French priest and philosopher Jean Buridan (1300–1358) is associated with the paradox (not attested in his received writings) known as "Buridan's ass": a wholly rational ass will starve if placed between two equal supplies of hay because it will have no rational grounds for choosing either.

[46] *A certain Sasha Abramian.* "Here Izdryk recreates the biography of a real person, one of his fellow students, Oleksandr Abramian. However—and this is typical of Izdryk—he demiurgically combines facts with his own inventions, and this alone explains the appearance of homosexual motifs in the chapter 'Awakenings Continued'" (Yeshkiliev, 18).

[47] *Freddie Mercury.* A British rock star of Indian parentage (1946–1991).

[48] *Tchaikovsky and Gide, Caravaggio, Mercury, Wilde and Kost Hnatenko.* "A list of notable creative figures also known for their homosexual orientation. The appearance in this set of world eminences of the Kyiv television journalist Hnatenko is, obviously, an example of Wozzeck's humor of alienation" (Yeshkiliev, 18).

[49] *"What a guy, writing all night, not a moment's rest, how very interesting and pallid!"* Yeshkiliev: "A quotation from the second-last chapter of Nabokov's novel *Despair*" (19). Nabokov's novel *Otchaianie* (1934) was translated by the author into English and published as *Despair* in 1937. Izdryk quotes verbatim in the original Russian. Nabokov used the prerevolutionary Russian orthography in the first Berlin edition; Izdryk transliterates this and other texts from Nabokov into the modern Ukrainian version of Cyrillic, strengthening the parodic quality of the quotations. For the passage used here (which occurs in the last, not the second-last, chapter), see Vladimir Nabokov, *Otchaianie* (Berlin: Petropolis, 1936; rpt. Ann Arbor: Ardis, 1978), 198.

[50] *Demiurges.* "Demiurge," the Greek word for "craftsman," was used by Plato to designate the maker of the material world. This is the primary sense in which the term is employed here. Demiurgy as the practice of the creative artist is also a central concept in the reflections of the Stanislav Phenomenon's chief theorist, Volodymyr Yeshkiliev: "In relation to literary texts the term 'demiurgy' is used to signify a specific approach to creating the artistic text where the author makes the plot, the structure and the discursive space of the literary work subordinate to the purpose of constructing a specific personal world that has its own physical, social and ideological rules, different from those that prevail in the existing world, and that is shaped by its own history.... Demiurgic practice demands that the author possess both external erudition (concerning the existing world) and inner erudition. Inner erudition means the fullest possible knowledge concerning the personal world created by the author and requires the construction within the literary work of an encyclopedia of this personal world." See Yeshkiliev, "Demiurgy," in *Mala ukraïns'ka entsyklopediia aktual'noï literatury* (Short Ukrainian Encyclopedia of Contemporary Literature) (Ivano-Frankivsk: Lileia-NV, 1998), 47–48. Yeshkiliev finds the principle of demiurgy best embodied in the works of J. R. R. Tolkien (1892–1973) and Jorge Luis Borges (1899–1986), as well as in the genre of fantasy. The form of Izdryk's *Wozzeck* is such as to justify the claim that the work was the result of a demiurgic creative process according to Yeshkiliev's definition of the term.

[51] *Some of them That One could even identify.* The list that follows pays homage to most of the better-known participants of the Ukrainian literary avant-garde of the 1990s. In some cases, the names are humorously distorted. "Irpinets" is a name formed by blending the surname of the poet, dramatist and member of the Bu-Ba-Bu group Oleksandr Irvanets (b. 1961) with the name of the town of Irpin near Kyiv. Two of the names are anagrams: "Borakne" of the surname of the poet and member of Bu-Ba-Bu Viktor Neborak (b. 1961), "Kamidian" of the surname of the poet Petro Midianka (b. 1958). Yeshkiliev (19) conjectures that the name "Dovhy" alludes to the poet Yaroslav Dovhan (b. 1956). Several names belong to real persons. The poet, prose writer and

critic Oksana Zabuzhko (b. 1960) was the author of the novel *Pol'ovi doslidzhennia z ukraïns'koho seksu* (Field Research into Ukrainian Sex, 1996), which provoked a mild literary scandal. The poet Oleh Lysheha (b. 1949) is noted for the influence upon his work of Chinese and other Asian world views and meditative practices. Oleksandr Hrytsenko (b. 1957), a poet, writer and critic, was one of the first practitioners of the academic discipline of cultural studies in Ukraine. The poets Stepan Protsiuk (b. 1964), Ivan Andrusiak and Ivan Tsyperdiuk (b. 1969) were members of the poetic grouping "Nova deheneratsiia" (New Degeneration). Semen Lybon and Yuri Pozaiak are the pseudonyms, respectively, of the poets Oleksii Semenenchenko (b. 1962) and Yuri Lysenko (b. 1957), members, with Viktor Nedostup (real name: Viktor Lapkin) of the poetic grouping "Propala hramota" (Lost Certificate). (The Ukrainian adverb *lybon'* [perhaps] and the conjunction *pozaiak* [insofar as] seldom occur in contemporary usage and, when they do, have a slightly comical effect.) "Luhosad" was yet another group of three male poets: Ivan Luchuk (b. 1965), Nazar Honchar (b. 1964) and Roman Sadlovsky (b. 1964). The group's name, which also means "meadow garden," comprises the first syllables of the three members' surnames. The highly regarded poets Vasyl Herasymiuk (b. 1956), Ivan Malkovych (b. 1961) and Ihor Rymaruk (b. 1958) were key figures in the generation that was sometimes labelled *visimdesiatnyky* (people of the eighties). The poet Oleksandr Bryhynets (b. 1962) also wrote on the theory of free verse. The poet Moisei Fishbein (b. 1946) emigrated to Germany in 1979, where he continued to publish his modernist poetry in Ukrainian émigré journals. *Avzhezh* (To Be Sure) was a literary journal in Zhytomyr, a regional center west of Kyiv. During the 1990s it published both innovative and traditional writing. The name that appears to be out of step with this group is that of Dima Tsyperdiuk, a musician and concert impresario who specializes in world music.

[52] *Death in Venice. Der Tod in Venedig* (1912), a novella by the German author Thomas Mann (1875–1955).

[53] *The bazaar in Chernivtsi.* The Chernivtsi Market near Ukraine's border with Romania is one of the country's largest.

[54] *Inferno in the Tower.* A reference to the film *The Towering Inferno* (1974), directed by John Guillermin and Irwin Allen.

[55] *Shadows in Paradise.* A reference to the novel *Schatten im Paradies* (Shadows in Paradise) by the German writer Erich Maria Remarque (1898–1970), published posthumously in 1971.

[56] *Lucy in the Sky.* "Lucy in the Sky with Diamonds" and "Fool on the Hill" (both 1967) are songs by the Beatles.

[57] *Islands in the Stream.* A novel by Ernest Hemingway, published posthumously in 1970.

[58] *Festival-that-is-always-with-you.* Izdryk alludes here to two texts. In Yuri Andrukhovych's novel *Recreations* "The Festival That Is Forever With Us" is the title of a "scholarly and theoretical conference" within the program of the carnival that is the main event of the plot. Ernest Hemingway's account of artistic life in the Paris of the 1920s, *A Moveable Feast*, published posthumously in 1964, was known in the Soviet Union through a translation into Russian titled *Prazdnik, kotoryi vsegda s toboi* (The Holiday That Is Always With You), published in 1965.

[59] *Climb the equestrian statue of Marcus Aurelius.* The famous second-century statue of the Roman emperor stood in the Campidoglio square in Rome until 1979. "Quoted here is an episode from the film *Nostalghia* [1983] by the [Russian director] Andrei Tarkovsky [1932–1986] where the hero, the mad Domenico played by Erland Josephson, publicly immolates himself" (Yeshkiliev, 20).

[60] *"His heart belonged to another woman."* "Another quotation from Vladimir Nabokov's [English-language] novel *Pnin* [1957]" (Yeshkiliev, 20). See Vladimir Nabokov, *Pnin* (Harmondsworth: Penguin, 1960), 36.

[61] *"Gracefully bearing her basket, a woman with hair the shade of honey and the name of a Spartan crosses the square."* According to Yeshkiliev (20), a quotation from the poem "Zhyttia ts'oho mista" (The Life of This City)" by Halyna Petrosaniak (b. 1969), which appeared in her collection *Park na skhyli* (Park on the Slopes, 1996).

[62] *Circus Vagabundo.* See Yuri Andrukhovych's poem "Tsyrk 'Vagabundo'" (The Vagabundo Circus) in his collection *Ekzotychni ptakhy i roslyny* (Exotic Birds and Plants, 1991), which, as Yeshkiliev (20) points out, was one of the few that Izdryk set to music.

[63] *Gertrud Boddenwier.* This annotator has been unable to find data on any person with precisely this name. It is possible that Izdryk had in mind the Austrian Jewish expressionist dancer and dance instructor Gertrud Bodenwieser (1890–1959), who emigrated to Australia in 1939.

[64] *Queen Margot.* Marguerite de Valois (1553–1615), Queen of Navarre and sister of three kings of France, was nicknamed Margot by her brothers. She led a tempestuous life and took many lovers. The historical novel *La Reine Margot* (1845) by Alexandre Dumas (1802–1870) inspired several films and the Russian television serial *Koroleva Margo* (Queen Margot, 1996).

[65] *Fifty-two sunny years (clarinets). Soniashni kliarnety* (Sunny Clarinets, 1918), the best known of the early collections of the poet Pavlo Tychyna (1891–1967), is commonly regarded as one of the most perfect lyrical anthologies in Ukrainian literature.

[66] *"Hand someone a pumpkin."* In the traditional courting ritual in rural Ukraine, the presentation of the suitor's representatives with a pumpkin signified the rejection of the proposal by the young woman's family.

[67] *The third part of the rivers was not made bitter.* Compare Revelation 8:10–11: "And the third angel sounded, and there fell a great star from heaven, burning as it were a lamp, and it fell upon the third part of the rivers, and upon the fountains of waters; And the name of the star is called Wormwood: and the third part of the waters became wormwood; and many men died of the waters, because they were made bitter."

[68] *"Cupola of the corner building, like a warrior's helmet."* "Another quotation from Halyna Petrosaniak's poem "Life of This City" (Yeshkiliev, 21).

[69] *Bolivar cannot carry double.* The last line of the short story "The Roads We Take" by the American writer O. Henry (1862–1910).

[70] *Zhivago. Doktor Zhivago* (Doctor Zhivago, 1957), a novel by the Russian poet and writer Boris Pasternak (1890–1960). It is not clear why A.'s father is compared to the central character of Pasternak's novel.

[71] *"Fortunately it is sugar, not salt."* A quotation from Nabokov's *Pnin* (88).

[72] *Timofei Pahlch.* Pnin's name and patronymic are Timofei Pavlovich. As Pnin puts it, "The pahtronymic has the ahksent on the first syllable and the rest is sloored—Timofey Pahlch" (*Pnin*, 86).

[73] *Bicycle race.* The title of a song released in 1978 by the British rock group "Queen."

[74] *Munchhausen's mare with its arse whittled away.* The German aristocrat Karl Friedrich Hieronymus, Baron von Münchhausen (1720–1797) was reputed to have told extraordinary tales of his adventures. These were collected and published in English by Rudolf Erich Raspe in 1785 as *Baron Munchhausen's Narrative of his Marvellous Travels and Campaigns in Russia* and were subsequently further embellished by various authors in the nineteenth century. One of the episodes tells of a wolf's attack on the horse drawing Munchhausen's sleigh. The wolf begins to devour the horse's hindquarters, which makes the horse gallop the faster.

[75] *Some* Easy Rider's *axe.* Dennis Hopper's film about hippie bikers, *Easy Rider* (1969), contains a shot of a "Muffler Man" holding a large axe. Muffler men are North American roadside advertisements, normally but not necessarily for mufflers, in the form of oversize fiberglass statues.

[76] *We Are the Champions.* Title of a song by Queen (1977).

[77] *The scene of the action was a department store where Anton had once worked as manager.* Yeshkiliev remarks that "Anton is Anatolii ('Anton') Seliukh, Izdryk's close friend, a businessman and philanthropist, who was a member of the group that began publishing *Chetver*. He really is the owner of a barely profitable shop like the one described in the following episode. He named it 'Wozzeck' after Izdryk completed the novel. The well-known artist Yaroslav Yaremak subsequently painted portraits of Büchner and Izdryk on the façade" (22).

[78] *Boborykin.* Petr Boborykin (1836–1922), a prolific Russian novelist in the realist manner, was noted for the tediousness of his work.

[79] *Accord.* According to Yeshkiliev, such an agency did in fact exist in Ivano-Frankivsk (23).

[80] *Sich Riflemen.* The Ukrainian Sich Riflemen, formed in 1914 as a Ukrainian unit within the Austro-Hungarian army, achieved a distinguished battle record against Russian forces during the First World War and were among the military formations that fought in 1918–19 on the side of the Western Ukrainian People's Republic and the Ukrainian People's Republic. Another unit bearing the name Sich Riflemen was formed as part of the Army of the Ukrainian People's Republic in 1917 and remained active until 1921. In disfavor throughout the Soviet period because they had fought for an independent Ukraine, the Ukrainian Sich Riflemen were celebrated anew when the Soviet Union began to liberalize in the late 1980s. In Lviv, an early center of the revival of Ukrainian national sentiment, 17 September Street, whose name commemorated the day in 1939 when Soviet troops first entered the city, was renamed in honor of the Sich Riflemen.

[81] *"Om!"* In Ukrainian, the words for "Om," the incantation used in Hindu devotion, and "ohm," the unit of electrical resistance, are the same.

[82] *Jan Saudek.* A Czech art photographer (b. 1935) whose works are much as described in *Wozzeck.*

[83] *"Velvet Mothers of the Universe."* Yeshkiliev (24) considers this to be "a play upon the names of three alternative cult music groups: 'The Velvet Underground' [active in the United States in 1965–73], 'Mothers of Invention' [United States, late 1960s] and 'Plastic People of the Universe' [a Czech rock band representative of Prague underground culture between 1968 and 1989]."

[84] *Second velvet revolution.* The Velvet Revolution is the name often given to the peaceful overthrow of the communist regime in Czechoslovakia in November and December 1989. It is not clear why Izdryk called it a "second" revolution, though he may have had the 1968 liberalization in Czechoslovakia, often referred to as the Prague Spring, in mind as the first.

[85] *Revolt-Revue.* Yeshkiliev believes the title to be a parodic allusion to the Czech underground periodical of the 1980s *Revolver Revue.* He suggests that the modification of the original name creates an English-language pun that plays upon two senses of the word "revolt": as a noun synonymous with "rebellion" and as a verb that means "to provoke disgust" (24).

[86] *Radio Liberty.* During the Cold War the broadcasters *Radio Free Europe* and *Radio Liberty*, funded by the Congress of the United States, transmitted programs designed for listeners behind the Iron Curtain. The two bodies merged in 1975 to form Radio Free Europe/Radio Liberty. Reduced in size and budget after the fall of the communist regimes of Eastern Europe, the organization shifted its headquarters from Munich to Prague in 1995.

[87] *Aline Maurois (nothing about her is of interest to our story except her name).* It is unclear why this name should be of interest to the reader. Yeshkiliev (24) speculates that it blends the names of two French writers, André Maurois (1885–1967) and François Mauriac (1885–1970).

[88] *International School of Ukrainian Studies.* The International Association of Ukrainian Studies, founded as a result of expanded contacts between Ukrainian scholars and their counterparts in other countries in the late 1980s, organized summer courses under this name in the early 1990s.

[89] *Mejlakh-ha-Mavet.* The name appears to be a hybrid of "Mejlakh," a Jewish name common in Ukraine and Belarus, and "malakh-ha-mavet," "angel of death" in Hebrew.

[90] *East European goyim.* Yeshkiliev surmises that Izdryk has confused the Hebrew term for non-Jew ("goy," plural "goyim") with "oleh," plural "olim," the term for Jews returning to Israel (24).

[91] *Buchach, Vitsebsk or Przemyśl.* Cities located today in Ukraine, Belarus and Poland.

[92] *Weinstock's pharmacy.* Nabokov's novella *Sogliadatai* (The Observer, 1938), translated into English as *The Eye* (1965), contains a character called Weinstock. Yeshkiliev points out that the two streets in the address that follows are taken from the satirical poem "Bal w operze" (Ball in the Opera House, 1936) by the Polish poet Julian Tuwim (1894–1953) as rendered into Ukrainian by the doyen of Ukrainian translators, Mykola Lukash (1919–1988). Lukash augmented a list of streets enumerated by Tuwim with an invention of his own, "Novo-Lukashivska" (New Lukash Street), thus playfully inserting his signature into the text. See Mykola Lukash, *Vid Bokkachcho do Apollinera: Pereklady* (Kyiv: Dnipro, 1990), 393.

[93] *Enkayveedeegestapo.* A neologism created by combining the Russian-language acronym NKVD (*Narodnyi komissariat vnutrennikh del* [People's Commissariat of Internal Affairs], the name of Stalin's secret police in the years 1934–46) and the German contraction Gestapo (*Geheime Staatspolizei* [Secret State Police], the name of the Nazi secret police in the years 1933–45).

[94] *The nationality rubric in the passport.* Soviet passports, while attesting to the Soviet citizenship of their bearers, also stated their nationality, by which was understood the person's ethnic origin. The passports introduced by independent Ukraine did not include this information.

[95] *Quantity had turned into quality.* A parodic reference to Marx's claim, in volume 1 of *Das Kapital* (Capital, 1867), that Hegel in his *Logic* had discovered "that merely quantitative differences beyond a certain point pass into qualitative changes" (Karl Marx, Frederick Engels, *Collected Works*, vol. 35 [London: Lawrence and Wishart, 1996], 313), and to Friedrich Engels's further elaboraton of the idea in *Anti-Dühring* (1878) and his posthumously published *Dialektik der Natur* (Dialectics of Nature, 1925).

[96] *Both Boyle and Mariotte.* The physicists Robert Boyle (1627–1691) in England and Edme Mariotte (1620–1684) in France showed in 1662 and 1676 respectively that the volume of a gas varies inversely with its pressure. This principle, known as Boyle's law in English-speaking countries, was referred to as the Boyle-Mariotte law in the Soviet Union and its successor states. Mariotte also discovered that the eye has a "blind spot" at the point where the optic nerve enters it.

[97] *The pitchweed, the hedgewort, the fret-me-not, the philotendril, the protuberose, the succubent.* Approximations of Izdryk's invented Ukrainian names for plants.

[98] *That the stars in the heavens were only one of the productions in God's theater.* A quotation, as Yeshkiliev (25) points out, from Andrukhovych's poem "India" as read at a public performance, but differing slightly from the published version (*Suchasnist'*, 1994, no. 5: 15).

[99] *Gay-Lussac*. The French physicist Joseph-Louis Gay-Lussac (1778–1850) studied regularities in the behavior of gases when heated and when combined.

[100] *Khomsky*. A recurring figure in Ivano-Frankivsk writings: a poet in Andrukhovych's *Recreations* and an underground theorist in some of Yeshkiliev's stories and mystifications. In the *Short Ukrainian Encyclopaedia of Contemporary Literature* Yeshkiliev attributes to Khomsky (a pseudonym, the reader is told, chosen in honor of the American linguist Noam Chomsky) the project of creating "Khomsky's language"—a language that is both "apophatic" and "opposed to signs in principle" (*Mala ukraïns'ka entsyklopediia al'ternatyvnoï literatury*, 115–17). Apophasis is a figure of speech in which the speaker brings up a subject for discussion by claiming that it should not be mentioned. Apophatic or negative theology seeks the truth of God by considering what God is not.

[101] *The great blind Jorge*. The Argentinian prose writer Jorge Luis Borges (1899–1986), an exponent of literary forms that draw attention to the uncertainties and contradictions in the relationship between art and reality, and in reality itself.

[102] *Solange Mariott*. The Polish science-fiction writer Stanisław Lem (1921–2006) included in *Doskonała próżnia* (A Perfect Vacuum, 1971), his collection of reviews of nonexistent books, a text purporting to review a certain Solange Mariott's *Rien du tout, ou la conséquence*.